ELISSA'S QUESTION

An Ancient Greek Mythological Adventure

by

Geoff Pridham

WISDOM PUBLISHING

CONTENTS

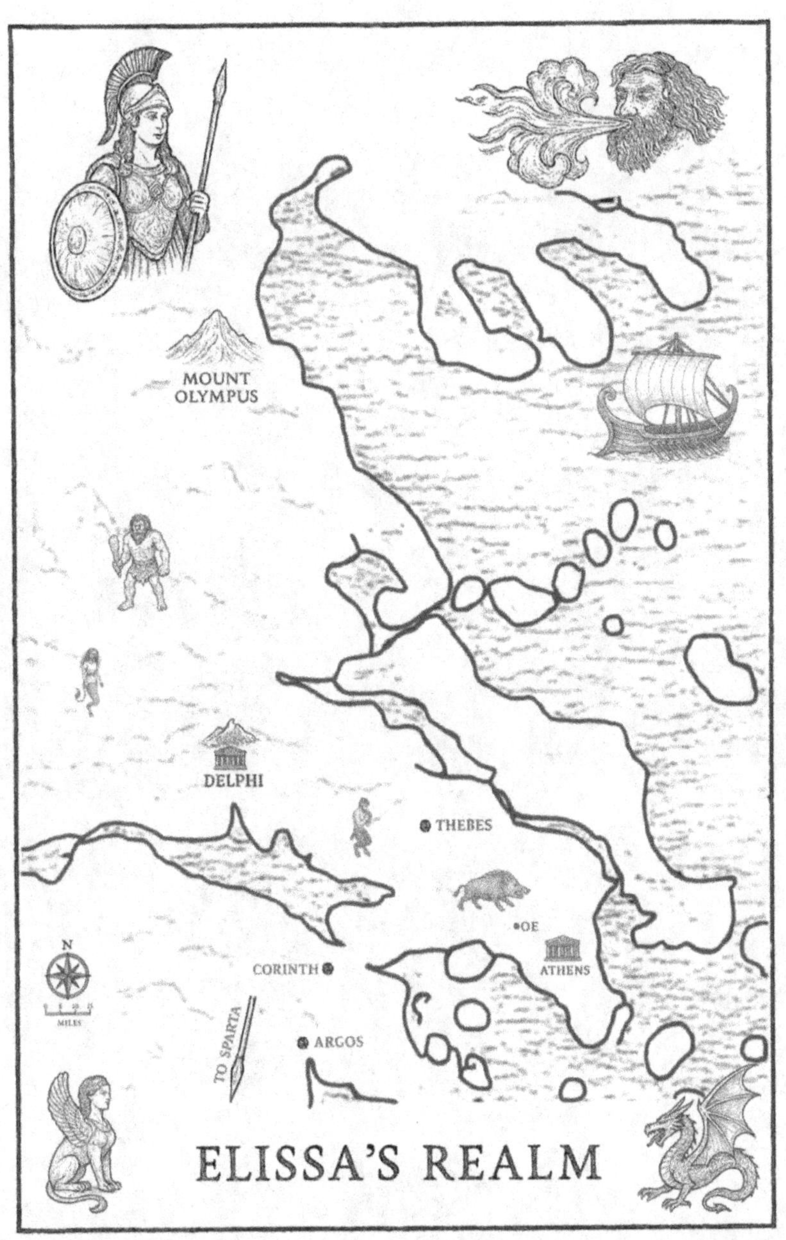

ELISSA'S REALM

1. ELISSA

Elissa was tired of hearing about marriage. Why did everyone say a kore had to get a husband? She wanted to keep living free, enjoying her life. Not be bound to a man and his household. Men! Why did everything have to revolve around men… and boys?

It was worse for slaves, though, Elissa had to admit. A woman may be tied to her husband, but at least she had some room for happiness in her life. Being a slave must be a nightmare, Elissa imagined. She admired her long dark hair in the bronze mirror. Slave women could not have beautiful long hair like this. Their hair was cut short.

Elissa stood up.

"Where are you going?" her mother, Agota, asked.

"Out," replied Elissa.

"A young lady should stay at home, in the gynaikon or the courtyard. She should not be 'going out,'" warned her mother.

"I know, Mother, but I have to take advantage of my freedom while I can," Elissa objected.

"I don't know what your father would say," complained Agota, "but go if you must!"

"Thank you, Mother," said Elissa, leaving the room.

Agota continued with her weaving.

Elissa went downstairs to the courtyard, picked up her hunting javelin and, covering her hair and face with a veil, left the house. She crossed the village and surrounding fields to enter the forest nearby.

Elissa enjoyed the freedom of running and hunting in the forest. Here she could practice her athletic skills without anyone criticizing her. She felt the weight of her hunting javelin as she balanced it in her hand, then tested how far and accurately she could throw it in the clearing. The warm fresh air rushed through her hair and across her face as she ran to get more momentum into the throws. If only she would have been allowed to do this at the Olympic Games! But women were forbidden from competing. Elissa had to practice alone, hidden from view in a forest.

After a few hours, Elissa saw that the sun was getting near the horizon. It would soon be dusk. She had better return home for dinner. She exited the clearing and left the forest, passing by fields where slaves tended the crops or looked after the sheep.

Making sure that her veil was hiding her hair and most of her face, she reentered the village and navigated through the streets to the house of her father, Yorgos.

Yorgos was a wealthy man in the Oe district and his house reflected that fact. It had two stories and an internal courtyard. Elissa hurriedly entered the courtyard via the front door and went to the bathroom to wash her feet. A house slave, Dora, brought her a cloth to dry them. Elissa left the bathroom and walked barefoot up the stairs to the gynaikon. Her mother and sister were there.

"Just in time for dinner," her mother said.

"Sorry, Mother," Elissa replied. She smiled at her little sister, Celandine, the youngest member of the family, in her first teen year.

"We have been weaving," Celandine said calmly.

"That's great," Elissa replied.

As it was the evening meal, they lay down on their individual klines to eat, rather than sit at the main table. The female slaves brought water in bowls for them to wash their hands. The slaves then placed food on the small three-legged trapeza tables next to each diner. Tonight they were eating cheese made from sheep's milk, bread dipped in olive oil, cucumbers, and beans. Agota drank watered-down wine from a shallow cup. The two sisters drank only water. Between the dishes they washed their hands in fresh bowls of water brought by the slaves. Dessert was nuts, figs and honey cakes. It was a good, tasty meal.

Elissa felt grimy after her practice in the forest, so she went downstairs to the bathroom to wash. In the courtyard she spotted her elder brother, Zotikos. He was a tall, older teenager, eighteen years old, with dark curly hair and a lithe, olive-skinned body.

"Hi, Zoti," Elissa called. "How was your day?"

"Hi, Elissa," Zotikos replied. "Quite good. We were learning some new songs today, and also practicing our military skills."

"I wish I could have joined you," said Elissa.

"You know that is forbidden," Zotikos replied. "Anyway, I can show you some of it later, if you like."

"Thank you, Zoti. I am off to wash now."

"Okay. I will join Father and Timaios for dinner. Good night."

"Good night, Zoti."

Elissa continued to the bathroom. Zotikos went to the andron to join the male members of the household. Dora brought Elissa some water from the courtyard cistern. Elissa smeared olive oil on her skin and then scraped it off with a bronze strigil. She finished washing by rinsing with the water, dried herself with a cloth, and then went upstairs to her bedroom to sleep.

The next morning, Elissa awoke and went along the upper story landing to the gynaikon to have breakfast with her mother and younger sister. They sat at the main table and had barley bread, which they dipped in a little red wine to make it softer. They also ate a few figs and drank water.

"After you clean your teeth and wash your faces we will be doing some weaving today," Agota announced.

"Yes, Mother," Elissa and Celandine replied.

They went downstairs to the bathroom to comply. Their father, Yorgos, saw them from the courtyard and called Elissa over. Yorgos was a mature man with much experience of life in the Attican farmlands near Athens.

"I want to talk to you, Elissa. About your future," Yorgos said.

"Yes, Father," Elissa replied.

"Come into my bedroom for a minute."

Elissa followed her father upstairs to his bedroom.

"Please sit," Yorgos pointed at a chair. "Now, you are a young kore well over the age of fourteen. It's high time you were married."

"Yes, Father. But is there no other way? I want to live free… and fight in a war, if needed," Elissa replied.

"A woman cannot live without a husband," Yorgos declared. "You know that. We have been over this before."

"Yes, Father. But it is so hard!"

"I understand," said Yorgos. "Perhaps it's all my own fault. I have been too easy with you over the years. But it is too late to go back now."

"I know, Father," Elissa sighed. "It is not your fault. It is my own restless nature, I guess."

"Yes, I guess so," Yorgos smiled. He gestured for Elissa to come over and gave her a quick hug.

"Don't worry. I will try to choose a good, easy-going husband for you. One you could stand. Go now and attend to your womanly duties with your mother."

Elissa nodded and left. In the bathroom she brushed her teeth with the frayed ends of a chewed stick dipped in tooth powder and washed her face before returning upstairs to rejoin her mother and sister. Although she had rinsed her mouth, Elissa could still taste the smoky flavor of the charcoal from the tooth powder for some minutes.

For most of the day the women got on with their weaving at their standing looms in the gynaikon.

In the afternoon, Agota went to check the house stores and instruct the slaves. The sisters could take a break from their work.

"Father says I should get married," Elissa said to Celandine.

"That is natural," Celandine replied.

"Yes," Elissa agreed. "But I don't want to go and live with some man."

"It wouldn't be so bad," Celandine said.

"For you, maybe. But it doesn't suit me."

"But what are you going to do?" asked Celandine. "Marriage is the right way to live."

"Maybe," said Elissa, "and maybe not."

"I worry for you," said Celandine. "I hope everything will be all right for you. Perhaps it will all work out!"

"One way or another, it has to," Elissa muttered.

"Elissa!" shouted someone from the courtyard.

Elissa went out onto the upstairs walkway to look. It was Zotikos.

"I can show you what I learned at the gymnasium. Lessons are over for today," Zotikos called.

"Great! I will ask Mother if I can go," said Elissa.

Agota gave Elissa permission and Zotikos and their younger brother, Timaios, left for the forest. Celandine stayed to help her mother with the women's work.

In the forest, Elissa felt alive. She laughed as she ran among the trees, taking deep breaths of the clean outdoor air, so refreshing after the stuffy atmosphere of the gynaikon. When the three got to the clearing, Zotikos showed Elissa and Timaios the latest he had learned about fighting.

"You must put on your best armor," he explained, "and take your spear and shield and line up with the other hoplites in formation. You lock your shields together and advance on the Spartans… or whoever the enemy is that day. Then you point your spear forward at them to impale them on the tip. If you are in the front rank, that is. If you are in the back rows you help push the front rank forward. Then you are true hoplites."

"I wish I could be there," said Elissa.

"You are a good fighter," Zotikos said, "but maybe not strong enough for the hoplites."

"I suppose not," agreed Elissa. "But I wish I could be."

"I could do it!" interjected Timaios. "I could be a hoplite!"

"One day. Of course you could," agreed Zotikos. "Keep up your training and in a few years you can go."

"I will!" Timaios declared.

"What about being a peltast?" Elissa asked. "I could bring my javelins and kill the Spartans with them."

"I'm sure you could," Zotikos replied, "but the battlefield is no place for women. In any case, you are too high-ranking to be a peltast. Father can afford better armor for you!"

"I guess so," Elissa agreed. "Show us what else you learned."

Zotikos explained that they had also been learning philosophy. Someone in Athens had been questioning the old ways and searching for the true good. He had asked many questions but no one could answer him.

Zotikos then taught Elissa and Timaios a new song. They all sang it together as they returned home through the forest and fields.

"Oh sons of the Greeks, go forward,
liberate the homeland,
liberate your children, your women,
the altars of your fathers' gods,
the tombs of your forebears,
now is the time to fight for everything!"

The siblings did not know that they had been secretly watched. A young man in dark green clothing had been observing them from among the trees. He quietly disappeared from view.

At home, Elissa washed and tidied herself then went upstairs for dinner. She joined Celandine and her mother for a pleasant meal of fish, bread and olives.

"Girls, there will be a symposium tonight," announced Agota, "so please stay out of the way. Timaios will be attending as he is old enough now."

"Timo can attend but not us," complained Elissa.

"Now, now," said Agota. "Enough of that. Prepare for bed and keep out of the way in your rooms."

"Yes, Mother," the sisters replied.

Celandine and Elissa washed themselves in the bathroom, said goodnight, and went upstairs to their separate rooms. It would not do to be seen by the men.

Elissa made sure her bedroom door was closed and lay on her bed for a while. She could hear the men arriving as they entered the andron for the symposium. As she had done many times before, she got down on the floor and carefully prized out a loose knot in the wood. It revealed a hole that did not go all the way through, but was deep enough for Elissa to be able to hear the conversation in the andron below. She dusted off the section of floor with her hand, placed her ear over the hole, and waited.

The men were still greeting each other as they lay down on their individual klines to eat and drink. Slaves brought them a variety of expensive and delicious dishes that they ate with their hands. The slaves also served them wine which had been mixed with water in a large decorated terracotta bowl that stood proudly in the center of the room. The guests congratulated Yorgos on the quality of the food and thanked him for his generosity.

"Not at all, my dear sirs," Yorgos replied. "You are all most welcome."

The flute girls had arrived and started to play. Beautiful tones wafted up to Elissa's ear. It must be fun to be in there, she thought.

"Business is good," one man said. "The harvest will be bountiful this year."

"With the help of the Gods, everything is going well," another man concurred.

Many murmured their agreement.

"We should get a good price in the market. I foresee us trading our olive oil for a huge quantity of grains. We should be well set to make bread far into the coming year."

"Yes, indeed."

"Not starving this year!"

"No!" everyone agreed.

"Thanks to Athena, we shall all do well again."

"Praise to Athena!"

"This wine is most pleasant, Yorgos," one man said.

"Thank you. It is made from my own grapes," Yorgos replied.

"Indeed. You have done a great job, as usual!"

"The crop was good this year. I am expecting to be able to supply many houses," Yorgos said.

"Put me down for some!"

"I will."

A few more requests to be remembered when the wine was ready for sale were made.

"I have produced some first-rate cheese," another man announced. "I will drop by and give you all some samples to try later."

"Excellent. Thank you," they all said.

There was more talk about food, trade and the general farming conditions. Then the discussion moved on to the slave situation.

"It's hard to get good quality slaves these days," one man said.

"Yes. And they cost too much," another agreed.

"I can't get them to work without watching them all the time," a third complained.

"Well, what can you expect from foreigners?"

"They are not tough like us," one said. "And not very smart either!"

"That's for sure!" another agreed.

"You've got to keep costs down, especially when you are considering the farm slaves," one man recommended. "They are only doing simple work and they can be happy with a simple life, so only provide the minimum that is needed for them to get by. Then your work will be done at the lowest possible cost, in spite of the fact that the slaves cost so much to buy in the first place."

"That's good advice," another agreed.

Elissa marveled at how the men spoke. They were so confident! It must be wonderful to be a man: deciding what to buy and what to grow, determining the future of our society. The world is theirs – to own and to rule!

The men were getting louder now. Even though their wine was mixed with water, they had drunk quite a few cupfuls.

"One way to get cheaper slaves is to capture them in battle," one man said.

"Do you think any battle is coming soon?" asked another.

"The Spartans can always be depended on to attack. They love causing trouble," stated a third.

"Sure. Anyone else?"

"The Persians may come after us again one day," said one man.

"We'll thrash them easily, all over again!"

Many loudly voiced their agreement: "Absolutely!" "No question!" "It will be a walkover!"

"I don't trust the Corinthians," one said.

"Nor do I," said another. "They are always after something."

"We will have to keep a close eye on them too!"

"Well, I hope we don't have to go to war too soon as I have to finish my harvest!" joked another.

"Me too! Not the best time for fighting!" one laughed.

There was some more eating and drinking while the men listened to the flute girls playing their cheerful tunes. Elissa took the opportunity to rest her ear, which was hot and sore from being pressed to the floor. After a time, the conversation resumed and Elissa pressed her ear to the knothole again.

"Have you heard about that ugly man in the Athen's agora? The one who talks a lot to everyone, asking them questions?" inquired one man.

"You mean Socrates?" another said.

"Yes, him. He keeps pestering people about their beliefs and what is 'the good.'"

"What's he going on about?"

"He says that he is trying to find out what is good: what is the right thing to do. He asks citizens to explain it to him, but then he often criticizes their answers."

"That sounds rude."

"Maybe. But he really does come across as sincere!"

"Okay. So what is his answer to the question… I mean, after he has finished bothering other people by asking them what they think?"

"He doesn't have one! He keeps saying he doesn't know the answer himself. He says that is why he is always having to ask everyone else."

"Well, I think doing the right thing is well known to be good," one man said.

"Maybe you had better go and answer him then! But I bet you he will have you questioning what you know by the time he has finished with you."

"I would tell him that doing what is right and being heroic in battle… and honoring the Gods, these are the things that make up 'the good.'"

"And restraining your passions and restraint in your style of living are important," one man added.

"Agreed," said the first man.

"But if you want others to do what is best for Attica then skill in convincing them is an important part of doing good," another man suggested.

"Yet I would argue that it is not a person's words that make them good, it is their actions," said one man.

"Obviously. But convincing others can lead to their actions also being good," the first man objected.

"I suppose so. There is some truth in that," the previous one conceded.

"Does 'the good' also apply to women and slaves?" a young man's voice asked.

"Of course not!" many replied. "Women and slaves cannot think, so the good cannot apply to them."

"How so?" asked the young man. "Could you please explain?"

"Certainly," one man said. "The good must apply to good action, which comes from good thoughts, and these come from good attitudes. If a person cannot think then how can they have good thoughts? Consequently, slaves, and to some extent women, cannot approach 'the good.'"

"Thank you, sir, for the explanation," the young man said.

"Call me Pavlos. We don't stand on ceremony here!" the man declared.

"Thank you, Pavlos. Could you tell me why slaves can't think?" the young man asked.

"Young man, that is something that you will know when you have to manage them!" Pavlos replied. "The Gods did not grant such people the ability to think, which is why you have to treat them like children and tell them everything that they need to do! They cannot be trusted with complicated matters, such as business. If you leave them alone they will just sit around and do nothing. You have to keep on their backs and ensure that your farm, or other business, is being attended to."

"I see, thank you for the explanation," the young man said. "Could you tell me in what way that applies to Attican women… and the other women of Hellas?"

"I will do it!" another man interjected. "Women have some ability to think. They are more like men than the slaves. But their abilities are limited. They can run the household and look after children, but above that they have no reliable abilities."

"Could they fight or compete in sports?" the young man asked. "What about throwing a javelin?"

The room burst into laughter.

"Of course not!" was the consensus.

"Then in terms of 'the good'?" the young man prompted.

"Since women's thinking ability must always be inferior to men's, it follows that they could never understand the idea of 'the good' fully. Consequently, the idea of 'the good' cannot fully apply to them, as they would never be able to grasp all of the concept," one man replied.

The room expressed agreement.

"I see," said the young man, and went silent.

Elissa wondered if the men really knew what they were talking about. She knew that she had the ability to think for herself, so why did they keep insisting that her ability was so limited? It didn't make sense.

"I wonder what Socrates would say about it?" one man said. "Maybe he would question *our* ability to understand 'the good'!"

"Knowing him, he probably would!" another man laughed.

Elissa considered if this Socrates would agree with the men at the symposium. Would he say that women could not think as effectively as men? Or would he ask them to explain how they knew that women cannot think to the same level? Maybe he would simply agree with their view. Or would he just say that he didn't know the answer himself?

Elissa speculated: What if men shouldn't really be running the world? How could we know if they are truly qualified?

Mostly men have the big muscles, she admitted, but does that necessarily mean that they make the best athletes? What if they let her put her athletic skills to the test? Wouldn't she be equal to some of the men? She bet she could even beat some of them, especially at javelin throwing!

Some of the Gods are female, like Athena and Hera. If the Gods can be female then why not some of the leaders of society? What made it different for mortals? After all, what is the true wisdom, who has it, where does it lie? What would that Socrates really say?

Elissa gave up on listening to the symposium. She carefully pushed the piece of wood back into the knothole in the floor, swept some dust over it to help conceal it, and went to bed.

The next day Elissa woke and went downstairs to the bathroom, where she washed her face and hands before breakfast. She returned upstairs and joined her mother and sister in the gynaikon. The three sat at the table and had breakfast together. After the meal they got back to their weaving. Several hours went by in silent work.

"Elissa," Agota said, "I think we should continue your training in running household affairs. Soon you will have a household of your own to run. You need to be ready!"

"Yes, Mother," said Elissa.

"Dora!" Agota called from the gynaikon entrance.

Dora came running.

"Yes, Mistress?" Dora said.

"Dora, fetch the household slaves here."

"At once, Mistress."

Dora ran downstairs and upstairs throughout the whole house to fetch everyone. The house slaves came running. The female slaves came into the gynaikon but the male ones stood back from the entrance with their eyes cast down.

"Good," said Agota. "Is everything in order? Are the tasks being done?"

"Yes, Mistress," they all replied.

"Excellent. My daughter and I will now check on your progress. You may return to your duties."

"Yes, Mistress," they said, and quietly left the area.

"We will first check the stores, Elissa," Agota said.

Agota led Elissa down the stairs and around the edge of the internal courtyard to the storeroom. The air felt colder in the windowless room. Inside were storage jars made from pottery. Agota kept the door open so they could see and went over to the huge jars, which were partly embedded in the ground to keep them cool. She opened their lids and looked inside.

"Plenty of olive oil left," Agota announced. "Barley getting a bit low – must buy some more. Wheat about half full – okay for now."

Agota gestured toward the smaller two-handled amphoras. "Please check those, Elissa," she asked.

Elissa went over to the amphoras. Some were sealed with cork stoppers and others were covered by lids. Elissa removed the stopper or lid of each one and looked inside, reporting what she saw.

"Plenty of honey – three amphoras. Wine running low after the symposium – we'd better get some soon!"

Agota and Elissa checked the other jars containing vegetables, fruit, and cheese and took note of what was needed. They then went to the kitchen to check the supplies and activities there. The numerous smells of the various items in the warm kitchen greeted Elissa's nose. The slaves were kneading dough on the kitchen table. Fruit was being washed. Vegetables were being peeled. Some fresh fish were being kept in cool water for the evening meal. The fire was burning in the hearth. All looked to be in order.

"We had better check the andron now," Agota said.

Agota and Elissa walked around the edge of the courtyard, keeping under the gables to avoid the sun. The men were away, so the pair went straight into the andron. There was still some mess from last night's symposium. Agota called a few of the house slaves in and ordered them to tidy up.

"That will be your job in future," Agota told Elissa. "I now ask you to check the rooms and instruct the slaves by yourself."

"Yes, Mother," said Elissa. "I will do it at once."

Elissa made a tour of the other rooms in the house and instructed the slaves to tidy up where needed. After checking their progress she returned to the gynaikon. Inside, the air had the odors of linen and dye. Agota and Celandine were at their looms, hard at their weaving.

"Elissa, please help us with the cloth," Agota instructed.

"Yes, Mother," Elissa replied. She stood with her mother and sister and helped them with the work. They were weaving an intricately patterned cloth that would be used to cover cushions for the klines in the andron. It was important for the andron to look its best for visitors to the household.

After a couple of hours of weaving, Agota remembered the wine.

"Elissa, you recall that we need more wine somewhat urgently? The slaves cannot be trusted to choose the best quality or negotiate a good price. Normally, I would go, but this time could you go and do your best for us?"

"Of course, Mother," Elissa replied.

Agota arranged for some strong male slaves to accompany Elissa and gave her a few coins.

"This should be enough for the wine," Agota said. "The slaves can carry the amphoras and also protect you. As the daughter of Yorgos, you should be accompanied by a suitable entourage."

"Yes, Mother," said Elissa.

Elissa changed into a fine peplos and donned a wide-brimmed straw hat to shield her face from the sun. She put on her sandals and went downstairs to join the slaves. They left the house and walked to the central area of the village.

In the bustling village Elissa was treated with respect. Citizens and slaves moved aside for her and her entourage. Elissa observed how the slaves were dressed. Most had simple clothes. The female slaves wore a plain peplos, similar to that of most of the women, but could usually be identified by their short hair. Wealthier free women had elaborate hairstyles, often adorned with jewelry. The best peploses had intricate colorful patterns, as did Elissa's.

The men were different. Male slaves often wore little more than a loincloth. Some were better dressed in short chitons. The free men also wore chitons of varying lengths and colors. The young men were happy to show off their strong healthy legs, while the older men usually covered themselves a bit more.

Elissa watched how the slaves were treated by the free people. The men strode around confidently, expecting slaves and women to defer to them. The women were more easygoing. They expected the poorer slaves to move aside, but did not seem to mind mixing with the better-dressed female slaves.

Elissa and her entourage arrived at the door to the wine merchant's store. One of her slaves opened it for her and she went inside.

"Good day. How can I help you, Mistress?" asked the merchant.

"Good day, sir. I would like to buy some wine. Good quality, but not too expensive," Elissa replied.

"How much do you need?"

"Two chous, please."

"Yes, Mistress. I have some fine wine just in. Would you like to sample it?"

Elissa was a little shocked by this invitation but decided to act calmly.

"Just a sip," she replied.

The merchant poured a small amount into a cup and gave it to Elissa. She tasted it carefully. It was sweet and aromatic.

"Yes, that will be acceptable," Elissa said. "How much are you asking?"

"This is a very fine red wine from Chios, so I have to ask for four drachmas," the merchant replied.

"That seems like rather a lot!" Elissa protested. "Could you make it better?"

"I could give you a cheaper, inferior wine, if that would suit you," the merchant replied.

"How about two drachmas for the good wine?" Elissa suggested.

"Agreed," said the merchant. He poured two chous of the wine into two small amphoras and sealed each with a cork.

Elissa gave the merchant two one-drachma coins. A couple of her slaves took the amphoras and Elissa and her entourage left the shop.

On the way home, Elissa again watched how the slaves were treated – the confidence and openness of the male citizens contrasted with the quietness and humility of the male slaves. Even the better-dressed slaves, who were probably farm managers or skilled workers, were quiet and humble. With the women it was a bit freer and easier. Well-dressed slaves were treated more equally, especially by the poorer-looking women.

The free women were always fully covered by their long peploses, but they still acted with a level of decorum among the men. The free men were loud and brash, looking in whatever direction they pleased, but the women were careful not to meet their gaze. "How different it is to be a man!" Elissa thought. She wondered if any of the men had noticed the way she was looking around, but then she muttered to herself: "I don't care what they think!"

Elissa arrived at her father's home. She instructed the slaves to put the wine in the storeroom and went up to see her mother.

"There you are, Elissa," Agota said. "How did it go?"

"Hello, Mother. I got the wine. Is two chous enough?" Elissa replied.

"Yes, that should do for now. Yorgos is not planning any symposiums for a while."

"I got wine from Chios. It was expensive," said Elissa.

"That is the best!" Agota agreed. "How much did you pay?"

"Two drachmas."

"Okay. Normally I would pay less," said Agota.

"Sorry, Mother. I am not that familiar with the price of wine. How much should I have paid?"

"Not much less. I would have tried for one drachma, but it does depend on how the wine tastes," said Agota.

"It seemed okay to me," said Elissa. "I guess."

"Not a problem. I look forward to tasting it later!" said Agota.

"I think I'll go and check the rest of the household now," said Elissa.

"Great idea," agreed Agota.

Elissa left the gynaikon and went to the walkway.

"Dora! Are you there?" Elissa called.

"Yes, Mistress," Dora replied, running over.

"There you are, Dora. I wanted to ask you some questions."

"Yes, Mistress?"

"Could you show me how you slaves live in our house?" asked Elissa.

"H-how w-we live?" Dora stammered.

"Yes, please."

Dora looked embarrassed. "We live very well, thank you, Mistress," she said.

"Sorry. I did not mean to distress you," Elissa said. "It's just that I am really interested. Could you show me where you sleep and what work you do?"

"Yes, Mistress," Dora said. She walked meekly along the walkway to a door. "We female slaves sleep in here," she said, opening the door and standing aside.

Elissa looked into the small room. There were a few cots squeezed on the floor for sleeping, leaving just enough space for a modest chest. She guessed that the slaves kept all their clothes and possessions in it.

"Thank you," Elissa said. "What work do you and the other slaves do around the house?"

"We help with the household chores – cooking, tidying up and cleaning," Dora replied. "We fetch the water and carry the food and supplies."

"I see. Who looks after the hearth? Who keeps the fire burning? Does anyone clean the statue of Hermes in the courtyard?"

"We do all that, along with the men," Dora replied.

"I see. There is a lot of work!" Elissa observed.

"Yes, Mistress."

"But you must have time off to eat and wash," Elissa said.

"Yes, Mistress."

"The water is heavy, isn't it? I remember going to the spring with some of the ladies when I was a girl. I could not lift the jars!"

"We are used to it, Mistress," Dora replied.

"You are used to it!" Elissa said. "I guess you are! But are you and the other slaves happy?"

"Yes, Mistress. We are all happy," Dora replied.

Elissa carefully studied Dora's face. "You are all happy? Are you sure?"

Dora lowered her gaze to the floor. "Yes, Mistress."

"Well, I am glad to hear that," said Elissa. But she was not so sure that it was true. "Thank you, Dora, for sharing your views with me. You may go back to what you were doing."

Dora nodded and left.

Elissa wanted to continue her investigation into the slaves' lives. After lunch, she asked her mother's permission to visit the farm with Zoti. Agota summoned Zoti and asked him if he would accompany Elissa on a visit to the farm. Zoti agreed and the two set off.

Elissa and Zoti soon arrived at the farm. Elissa could see the familiar groves of her father's olive trees stretching along the hillsides. There were fields where sheep were grazing. Shepherd slaves were watching over them. Elissa knew that there were also fields of barley and smaller plots of vegetables, such as cucumbers, lettuce, garlic, onions and broad beans. Her father also had some small orchards with pear, fig and apple trees. Finally, he grew some grapes for his own wine production. Maybe it was not as good as Chios wine, but Elissa remembered that her father and his friends said they liked it!

Elissa and Zoti walked among the fields. Male slaves were hoeing and weeding in the full glare of the sun, without hats and wearing only loincloths. It looked like hot, thirsty work. Elissa and Zoti passed the slaves and continued walking. They approached the main farm buildings. Next to the buildings there were pens of pigs. Chickens roamed freely. Some citizen farm workers were repairing a pig pen, assisted by a few slaves. Zoti waved to them and they waved back.

"Good day, Master Zotikos," some said.

"Good day, all," Zoti replied.

The workers nodded and continued with their repairs.

"So, here we are," Zoti said to Elissa. "What did you want to see?"

"Could I see where the slaves live?" Elissa asked.

"Of course," Zoti replied. "This way." He led Elissa to the farm buildings.

Inside the largest building there were stalls for animals, workshop areas, and rooms for the slaves. Elissa looked into one of the rooms. Its dirt floor was lined with simple reed mats for the slaves to sleep on. In the next room there were a few olive-wood chests where the slaves kept their meager belongings. The room also contained a basic wooden table and benches where they could eat.

Elissa and Zoti crossed to the next, smaller building. Inside, there was a shared bedroom for the female slaves with a separate food preparation and eating area. Elissa checked the slaves' provisions. They included barley, cheese, eggs, olive oil and vegetables. She could not see any meat or fish. There was water but no wine. For dessert there were some figs and nuts, but no honey.

"Is this all they eat, Zoti?" Elissa asked.

"Sure. They make bread too," Zoti replied casually.

"But is there any fish or meat?"

"I don't know. I think they get some fish and chicken from time to time," Zoti said.

"But how can they have enough energy to do their work? How can they keep healthy?" Elissa asked.

"They're okay," Zoti said. "They get their work done."

"Why do they have to live like this? It doesn't seem right!" Elissa complained.

"Elissa, this is how they are meant to live," Zoti replied. "They are used to it. They don't mind at all."

"Are you so sure, Zoti? How can you know that?" Elissa demanded.

"It's not as bad as you think, Elissa," Zoti replied. "You don't know normal life. Many Atticans live like this… and they are free!"

"They do?"

"Yes. Not everyone has a nice two-story house! Plenty have just two rooms to live in. And they can't afford meat, or wheat for bread. They eat straight barley bread. Plenty of people like that work here on Dad's farm. And they are not slaves. You see: our slaves are not that badly off. Dad treats them well," Zoti claimed.

"So this is a good life!" Elissa said. "I wonder."

Zoti looked at his sister. "Anyway, why are you so interested in this all of a sudden? Is it because you are preparing for marriage? You want to know how to run your own household?" Zoti asked.

"It's nothing like that!" Elissa replied. "I am just interested, that's all. I am not planning anything!"

"Okay, okay. Keep your chiton on!" Zoti said. "I was just curious."

"Sorry, Zoti. Thanks for bringing me here," Elissa replied in a calmer tone.

"No problem, Elissa. Any time," Zoti said.

"Let's go home, Zoti," Elissa said.

Elissa and Zoti left the farm buildings and walked back to their house. Elissa thanked Zoti again and went upstairs to the gynaikon. Celandine was alone, getting the table ready for dinner.

"Hello, Celandine," Elissa said.

"Hello, Elissa," Celandine replied.

"I have just been up at the farm with Zoti," Elissa said.

"Oh yes? What were you doing up there?" Celandine asked.

"I wanted to see how the slaves live… how they are treated."

"Yes?"

"You should see it. They all sleep in one room on mats on the floor!" Elissa said. "It was horrible. And they have to eat simple food. They never get fish or meat… or maybe rarely, I am not that sure."

"But they are doing the work okay, aren't they?" Celandine asked, as she finished setting the table.

"Sure. Of course they are, I expect. But they shouldn't have to live like that!" Elissa complained. "Zoti seemed to think it was all right, though. He said other Atticans live worse than that."

"Probably," Celandine commented. "Anyway, what has this got to do with us? Isn't the running of the farm a men's affair?"

"Maybe it is," Elissa replied. "But it still bothers me anyway!"

Celandine shrugged. "You are older and wiser than me, sister. I only know how to do home things. I will let the men take care of men's affairs when I grow up, but I don't know how that is going to work for you!"

"No. Me neither," Elissa smiled.

Agota returned from the kitchen. The sisters greeted her and got on with arranging the room for dinner. This was not the right time for a discussion about men's affairs!

During dinner, Elissa wondered what her mother really felt about her life here. Was she aware of the stifling limitations, or didn't they bother her? How could Elissa find out? Elissa didn't want to offend her mother. There just didn't seem to be any polite way to ask. She sighed and went on eating.

The next day passed in a similar way to the day before. Washing, breakfast, weaving. Household chores and organization. Checking the stores. Lunch.

After lunch, Elissa quietly left the gynaikon, crept downstairs, slipped on her sandals and, checking that no one was looking, snuck across the courtyard and into the street. She proceeded in the direction of the farm. She wanted to know more about the life there, but figured that her mother and father would not readily agree to letting her go again.

As Elissa neared the farm she saw a group of wild boars on the road. She stopped and stood completely still, but the boars approached and surrounded her. Most of them seemed to find her harmless, but one of the males appeared angered by her presence. He glared at her through his small dark eyes. Elissa stood as still as she could and tried to imagine that she was invisible. The boar did not care. He definitely did not like this human intruder.

A slave was working in the field nearby and saw what was happening. He dropped his hoe and began to run over.

Elissa wished that she had brought her hunting javelin with her, or at least a knife! The boar growled and worked its jaws. Foam appeared around its mouth. Suddenly it charged, its sharp tusks aimed straight at Elissa. Surrounded by boars, she had nowhere to run. She faced the boar resolutely. It was almost upon her. The slave arrived and jumped in front of her. The boar hit him hard, savaging him with its razor-sharp tusks. Bright red blood gushed out of the slave's legs and chest. He fell to the ground.

Some other slaves had seen what was happening and came running, waving their arms and shouting at the wild boars. The boars were disturbed by all the commotion and started to scurry away. The vicious male boar ceased his attack and followed them.

Elissa knelt beside the wounded slave.

"Thank you for saving me," Elissa said. "What is your name?"

"Kepheus," the slave sputtered. "I hope you are all right, my Mistress," he said, and then died.

Elissa cradled his head gently in her arms. "Good night, Kepheus," she said. "Rest well."

The other slaves had arrived. They bent and helped Elissa to her feet, then led her away from the blood-soaked body, making sure that she did not look back.

"Shall we take you home, Mistress?" one of the slaves asked.

"But what about Kepheus?" Elissa replied.

"We will take care of him later, but first let us get you home, Mistress," the slave said.

Elissa nodded and the slaves helped her to walk home. Yorgos was in the courtyard.

"What's happened here?" Yorgos asked, stepping forward.

"Mistress has had some trouble," one of the slaves replied.

"Elissa? What happened?" Yorgos asked.

"I was saved from a wild boar," Elissa sobbed. "Kepheus jumped in front of it and saved me."

"That was good of him," Yorgos said. He gazed at the slaves. "Where is he now?" he asked them.

"He has died, Master Yorgos," they replied.

"I see. Thank you for bringing Mistress Elissa home," Yorgos said.

The slaves bowed.

"Now go and bury the body... away from the village and living quarters," Yorgos instructed.

"Yes, Master Yorgos," the slaves replied and left.

"But you don't understand, Father. He saved my life!" Elissa cried.

"That was his duty," Yorgos replied. "He has done what he ought to do." He looked carefully at Elissa. "You have blood on your clothes. Are you all right? Are you injured?"

"I am fine," Elissa mumbled. "I am uninjured. That is Kepheus's blood."

"I am glad," Yorgos said. "You had me worried. You had better go and wash and change," he advised.

"But what about Kepheus? Who will take care of him?" Elissa sobbed.

"You have had a shock. Those wild boars have been a menace lately. I will talk to the village leaders about them. We need some action," Yorgos replied.

"And Kepheus?"

"The slaves will take care of him. He is one of theirs," Yorgos answered. "Now go and change."

"Yes, Father," Elissa said, and went to the bathroom.

Dora assisted Elissa, bringing her a fresh peplos to change into.

After washing and changing, Elissa went upstairs to her room. She felt ashamed that she had caused the death of Kepheus. She couldn't get it out of her head. If she hadn't sneaked out to her father's farm then none of this would have happened. Kepheus would still be alive, happily hoeing his field in the sun. If she had stayed at home, dutifully attending to women's business, then Kepheus would be unaffected. Life on the farm would have gone on unchanged… undisturbed by her foolishness. Her unrestrained curiosity had led to his death!

This was the first time Elissa had seen someone die. It was all over so quickly! One minute someone was alive, going about their daily business, then suddenly their blood was gushing out everywhere in a bright red stream and they were dead. It was all over for them. The underworld awaited their soul's imminent arrival.

Agota knocked on the door and entered Elissa's room.

"How are you, my dear?" Agota asked. "I heard what happened. Are you all right?"

Elissa looked up from her tear-soaked pillow. "I am unharmed," she replied. "Though Kepheus is dead because of my willful stupidity!"

Agota came over and sat beside Elissa on the bed. She patted her and said: "There, there. It is not your fault. We all know how curious you are about the outside world, but it is not your fault that the wild boars were there at that time."

"I know, Mother. I know. But if I hadn't gone and had stayed at home, like you said, then none of this would have happened!"

"Perhaps," Agota agreed, "but how can you know what the Gods had in mind? Maybe they planned all this for some purpose of their own. How can we mere mortals know?"

Elissa looked confused.

"Why don't you put this out of your mind for the time being and come to dinner?" Agota suggested.

"I can't eat right now, Mother," Elissa replied. "I am too upset. I don't have any appetite."

"Then get some rest, my dear," Agota advised. "Try to sleep. It will all look better in the morning, I promise you."

Agota stood up and left the room, gently closing the door behind her.

Elissa lay back on her pillow. If only she hadn't gone to the farm in secret. Things would be so much better now. If she hadn't had to hurry out of the house she may have taken her hunting javelin. Maybe that would have changed things. Or maybe not. Maybe if she had stayed at home, as a young woman should… her thoughts went round and round. Eventually, she fell asleep.

As Elissa slept, she dreamed about the life of slaves and wild boars. Sometimes the boars attacked and sometimes they were peaceful. The slaves worked hard in the sun, sweating and suffering in silence. Sometimes the boars attacked them, but the slaves shooed them away with their hoes. One time a slave used his hoe to catch a boar by its tusks and flick it into the air, using some kind of magical lever action. Another time the boars surrounded a slave and crushed him to death. Bright red blood went spurting everywhere. This vision woke Elissa.

It was dark in the room. Elissa wondered how long she had been asleep. Thoughts came to her mind: How can I justify myself and my way of life? Why didn't I accept marriage before, when I was younger? Why didn't I do as I was told? Why haven't I followed the ways of a normal kore? Then none of these bad things would have happened. She realized that this didn't make sense. These thoughts were getting her nowhere. She would need to seek better guidance than these were providing!

Elissa struck a piece of steel against her flint-stone, directing the resulting sparks onto a tuft of tinder. She took the little bundle into her hands and gently blew on it until it started to burn, then carefully used the burning tinder to light the wick of her oil lamp. By the light of the lamp, she searched inside her clothes chest for her finest peplos and changed into it. She brushed her hair carefully and crept downstairs to the bathroom to wash her face and hands, out of respect for the Gods.

The rest of the household was asleep, so Elissa tiptoed as quietly as she could to the family's courtyard shrine to Athena. She stood humbly before the small statue of the goddess and prayed silently for guidance. When she had finished praying, she hung a gold necklace on the hand of the statue as an offering.

Elissa returned upstairs to sleep. This time her dreams were about Kepheus and his noble sacrifice to save her.

In the morning, Elissa awoke, washed her face, and went up to the gynaikon for breakfast. She still did not feel hungry but ate a little bread with olive oil so her mother would not worry.

Agota asked Elissa how she was feeling today. Had the night's rest cleared her mind?

"I am all right, Mother," Elissa answered.

"I was worried about you when you couldn't have dinner, but it is good to see you up and eating again," Agota said.

"Thank you, Mother," Elissa replied.

"That's all good then," Agota observed.

"Yes, Mother. But I wonder what Kepheus would be doing now… if all that hadn't happened."

"Kepheus was the slave?" asked Agota.

Elissa nodded.

"Well, I expect he would be performing his duties," Agota said.

"Mother, I am grateful for your concern about me, but don't you care about Kepheus at all?" Elissa protested.

"Of course I do!" Agota complained. "But it is over now and there is no use going on about it. The important thing is that you are okay."

"Yes, Mother," Elissa said dully.

Agota studied Elissa's face carefully. "Elissa, listen to me. It is the duty of slaves to serve and protect their masters and mistresses. Kepheus, if that was his name, has done just that. He is to be honored for doing his duty. It is good that you feel gratitude for what he has done. Respect that feeling. It will give you the strength to carry on with your life."

Elissa thought about this advice. She wondered if Athena would say the same thing. Perhaps her prayers would be answered one day and she would know.

"Actually," Agota continued, "I think it might help if you return to normal life. Then you will forget all your worries and feel better. You should focus on your weaving for today."

"Very well, Mother. I will do as you say," Elissa assented.

After breakfast, Elissa remained with Agota and Celandine in the gynaikon and quietly helped with the spinning and weaving.

Later that morning, Yorgos sent word to Elissa, asking her to join him in the andron. Elissa left her work and went downstairs to meet him, expecting he would want to discuss the death of Kepheus.

Yorgos invited Elissa to sit on one of the klines near him.

"Good morning, Elissa. I hope you are feeling better today," Yorgos began. "I have asked you here to talk about your marriage," he continued. "We need to consider who would be suitable."

Elissa was shocked. Could her father really be discussing marriage the day after Kepheus was killed? It seemed impossible. What could it mean? Perhaps it was because Kepheus would still be alive if she had already gotten married. She wouldn't have been around to cause trouble. Could that be why? She decided to ask him.

"No, that is not the reason, Elissa!" Yorgos replied. "It's nothing like that. I don't know how you could have thought that. Look, you shouldn't be worrying about the slave. He was doing his duty. It could have happened in his defending anyone at any time. It had nothing to do with what happened yesterday. If you hadn't gone to the farm by yourself then someone else could have been trapped by wild boars and attacked on a different day. You don't need to give it a moment's more thought." He paused to consider. "You know what I think? I think that if you focus on your potential marriage, who would be suitable for you, then that will redirect your attention to more fruitful matters. What do you say?"

"Yes, Father. I think you are right," Elissa replied. But inside she felt dismayed. So this is how it is, she thought.

"Good girl. You know: 'Life goes on under the Gods,'" Yorgos advised.

Elissa returned to the gynaikon and rejoined the spinning and weaving. Cloth was always needed.

For the rest of the day, Elissa tried to focus on the daily life concerns of women. She kept feeling that the death of Kepheus was caused by her own disobedience. Focusing on what women were supposed to focus on seemed like the best way to make up for that. After all, if she hadn't been meddling in men's affairs then none of this would have happened.

In the afternoon, Elissa accompanied her mother when she went to instruct the household slaves. Elissa then walked alone to the storeroom to check the stores by herself. She noted that the ordinary daily drinking wine that her mother had ordered had not arrived yet. This would need to be followed up with the merchant.

Elissa thought about what else might be needed in the household. Would she be able to work it out without assistance? She looked around the storeroom, checking what types of things were kept there. What produce was in the amphoras and pithos? What else was stored in the room? She went to the kitchen and asked some of the household slaves what supplies should be stored in the storeroom and how much of each was needed. They answered shyly, especially as they were speaking to the mistress's elder daughter, but everything they said made sense.

The next day came and Elissa arose and went down to wash her face and hands before breakfast. In the gynaikon she forced herself to eat normally, as if nothing had happened. What activities would they have today? Obviously there were no little children to look after anymore, her sister and brothers were too old for women's care, so today their activity would be to weave intricately patterned cloths. This should keep the women occupied while they stayed out of the sun, locked away inside their home!

Elissa thought about checking the stores again, but then remembered that she had already done this yesterday. She asked her mother what she could check now. Agota advised her to check the men's rooms as they were all out doing men's things. The rooms may need some cleaning or rearranging.

Elissa took Agota's advice and checked her brothers' and father's bedrooms and then went downstairs to check the andron. Some of the house slaves accompanied her, but they had been tidying up already, so there wasn't much to do. The bedrooms were similar to her own, with a simple bed, a chair and a chest. The andron was more glamorous, with its colorful mosaic-tiled floor, decorative wall hangings, beautifully-patterned kline covers, three-legged side tables, small marble and bronze statues, and tall bronze lampstands. Elissa marveled at the luxuriousness of the room. It must be wonderful to meet in here with all the other men and talk business and philosophy, she thought.

Suddenly she became aware of the slaves standing near her. What did they think of all this opulent pleasure still going on after the death of Kepheus? She felt like a hypocrite: admiring the andron… this style of living! What must the house slaves think of them: the privileged owners who carried on like nothing had happened, like the world was still a happy, pleasant place? She felt her face burning in response to their imagined contempt. She could not stand it any longer. She ran out of the room and into the courtyard, grabbed her hunting javelin and sandals, and rushed out of the house. She avoided the farm and was soon back in the forest clearing.

Elissa tried practicing her javelin throwing. She made a few throws, but the joy had gone out of it. It was not making her feel better at all. She sank to the ground, experiencing remorse for what she had done to Kepheus. What kind of a woman was she?

Elissa's younger brother, Timaios, came into the clearing. He waved to Elissa and walked over.

"Hi, Elissa!" Timaios said.

Elissa nodded back.

"I heard about your big adventure the other day. What was it like? How come you didn't kill the boar yourself?" Timaios asked eagerly. He sat down beside Elissa.

"I couldn't, Timo. I didn't have my javelin with me… or even a knife! I was surrounded by other boars. It all happened so fast. There was nothing I could do," Elissa replied.

Timaios nodded. "I understand. When you are in the countryside you should carry your weapons with you at all times!"

"I guess that would help," Elissa agreed, pointing to her javelin.

Timaios nodded enthusiastically.

Elissa and Timaios talked for a while and later returned home.

The next day Elissa decided that she should go back to women's duties. Her escape to the forest clearing yesterday had not been wise, and it had not made her feel any better! She might as well get on with doing what women are supposed to do with their lives.

The day rolled on: eating, spinning, weaving, instructing the slaves, checking the stores… the usual routine. Elissa tried to take an interest in the beautiful intricate pattern that her mother was crafting on her loom. Agota certainly had the skill. Years of practice explained some of it, but she also had an artistic flair all of her own. Funny that men said women could not think when they could do work of this level, Elissa mused.

Elissa asked her mother how she worked out a pattern like that and what techniques she used to weave it. Agota showed her how she designed a pattern by drawing her idea with makeup chalk on a wooden board. As she did not know how to write, Agota had created her own symbols for the colors she planned to use. Agota then obtained the necessary dyed threads, either by spinning and dying them herself, or instructing the slaves to do it. When a sufficient length of each colored thread was ready, Agota would weave them into the required pattern at her standing loom. She showed Elissa how to prepare the warp threads, tying terracotta weights onto their ends to keep them vertical. Then, the warp threads were alternately placed on either side of the lower shed-rod. Some of the threads were tied via loops of string to the higher placed heddle-bar, depending on which side the horizontal weft thread was planned to pass. The heddle-bar was rested on the base of two forked sticks that were inserted into holes on each side of the frame of the loom. A shuttle was used to pass the appropriate weft thread through, then the heddle-bar was moved outward to rest in the forks of the forked sticks. This reversed the position of the alternating threads. The shuttle was then passed back through the warp threads in the opposite direction. To complicate matters, the weft threads had to be changed for each color needed, according to the design, and even which warp threads the weaver had to pass the shuttle through varied in order to get the required pattern. Sometimes the threads were prepared by twisting different colored ones together in precisely the correct lengths. Agota worked out all these details in her head as she went.

Elissa tried her best to emulate Agota's experienced technique. For a while she lost herself in the work of designing and weaving her own pattern. Time seemed to pass more quickly.

After lunch, Elissa went downstairs to check the storeroom once more. The ordinary daily drinking wine had arrived. Little else seemed to have changed, but she checked every single item in the storeroom again anyway. After all, she wouldn't want a symposium for the men to get underway, only to find that they had run out of treats! That would never do.

Elissa told herself that she would make a good wife now. She would attend to her husband's new household diligently and carefully, as she was doing in her family's home. There would be quality food on the table, delicious treats for his symposiums, lovely woven covers on the cushions and klines, and everyone happy and orderly. Hopefully, they would live close to her old family home, so she could visit her mother, sister and brothers often.

Elissa went into the courtyard and sat for a while. She imagined what it would be like when the children arrived. It was a little frightening to think of getting pregnant and giving birth, but her mother had done it, so why couldn't she? After they were born, she would have to look after them in the gynaikon on her own… or mostly on her own. She would see to their early education, nurse them when they were sick, ensure they were well-clothed, feed them, wash them, guide them in life's values. At least this would give her something to do during the day! She would not be bored. Or would she?

Elissa got up and went back into the storeroom to check the stores again, but nothing had changed. She went into the kitchen and checked how the slaves were preparing the food. She wanted to help but, as her father's was a wealthy household, the work was mainly for the slaves. She left the kitchen and went across the courtyard to check the andron, but the male slaves stood in her way and would not let her enter as the boys were back home. She went upstairs to the gynaikon. Inside, her mother and sister were still quietly weaving. Elissa went over to her loom and continued with her design.

As she toiled at her loom, Elissa started to realize something: "This is not working for me. I am not suited to this lifestyle. I am way too restless…"

Yorgos took time off from managing his farm to visit the important members of the Oe village community and nearby area. He could not afford to delay his search for a suitable husband for Elissa. She was clearly past the normal age for marriage of fourteen. Time had well and truly run out. If Yorgos didn't act now then it would be too late. Elissa would have to stay at home, alone and unmarried, trapped in his household for the rest of her life.

Yorgos hoped that he could find the right person within the village or its surroundings. It would be a great shame if Elissa had to move away to somewhere like Athens. Even though they might be able to visit her occasionally, he, and no doubt the rest of the family, would miss her terribly. Much better to find the partner-to-be in Oe.

It was not going to be an easy mission, however. Yorgos knew that. He realized that Elissa would make a difficult wife. She was so headstrong! Perhaps it was his own fault for indulging her whims when she was growing up. Or perhaps it was because she had two feisty brothers. Yet young Celandine was not like her. Celandine seemed quite happy with her lot. No, it looked like Elissa was just one of those girls who naturally grew up wanting more out of life. Maybe something like a man's life? Anyway, it made his work in finding her a suitable husband just that bit harder.

In any event, whichever way you looked at it, the fact was that the time was up!

Yorgos visited the finest houses in Oe and its surrounds, sounding out the views of the most respectable and valued citizen fathers. Would they favor an alliance with Yorgos's household? Would their sons agree? Could trade relations be improved by family connections? What were their thoughts on that?

Yorgos also invited the citizens to his own home and entertained them in the andron. It wouldn't hurt to give them some fine food and drink. That way, they would be able to fully apprehend the practical benefits of being allied with Yorgos! He even found some Chios wine to tempt them with. It was fortunate that Agota had thought to buy that. His respected gentlemen guests appreciated its sweetness on the palate and were also favorably influenced by its stronger level of alcohol.

Dealing with the fathers was one thing, but Yorgos was well aware that he would also need to assess the suitability of the sons. Even if a wealthy father would make a good connection for the future, a son who could not appreciate Elissa's unique nature may lead to a souring of the parents' "special relationship." Better to choose a son who was, how could he put it?, *more flexible* in his outlook. And even if the son was more flexible, there was always Elissa's view to consider. Mightn't she consider a flexible son to be *too* flexible? She was a strong woman – she might only favor a strong man. Yorgos needed to find a strong man who was also flexible about the strength of his woman!

Aware of these delicate needs, Yorgos entertained the fathers and subtly interviewed the sons, trying to divine how they might react to a daughter like his. What did the son expect from a wife? What functions would he want her to perform? What would be her duties in his household? Would she be permitted to go on journeys with him? A surprise question there. Was there any flicker of dislike in the son's eyes when asked such a thing? Yorgos watched carefully. If there was any sign of a problem, he crossed that candidate off his list. In this way, Yorgos explored and tested and chose.

Yorgos had his daughter's interests at heart. He knew what she wanted out of life, but he also knew that she had to move on and get married, no matter what shortcomings remained in his final list of candidates. That was the reality. He would do his best for her within the limits of what was practically achievable in the real world. This was all that he could hope to do.

As Yorgos made his rounds among the better homes in the village and surrounding area, a young man was watching him. He followed unobtrusively among the people. Yorgos never saw him.

Later, the young man went into one of the fine houses that Yorgos had visited. He did not come out again.

Elissa was lying on her bed and thinking. She could not sleep. All these bad events and the horrible future that awaited her were becoming overwhelming. She wondered why the Gods allowed these terrible events to happen. What were they thinking?

What do the Gods really want from us mortals? Do they care at all? Or are they wrapped up in their own immortal lives? Perhaps we are too small and insignificant for them to worry about. After all, what are we compared to them? We are like tiny insects. Why would a god care about what happened to tiny insects?

On the other hand, the Gods must have some plans for us. Wouldn't they want us to live in the right kind of way? What would be the true lifestyle that they would want? How would we know it if we saw it? For example, was it really true that a free Hellas woman should be the virtual slave of her father and then her husband? How would we know if that was what the Gods wanted? Or could it be that this role was made up by men? It was difficult to be sure.

As she pondered these perplexing questions, Elissa drifted off to sleep.

The next morning Elissa awoke and felt that her thoughts of the night before had been silly. It was probably all the stress of recent events that had made her think this way. As soon as she settled down and returned to normal life she would feel better. Her thoughts would align once again with what society considered best.

Elissa got up, washed her face, and went to breakfast in the gynaikon with Agota and Celandine. Here, at least, were two people who were clear on what a normal life should be like!

Elissa felt relieved that she had seen through her recent foolishness. A woman's life was well laid out by the Gods and the community. Elissa was ready and prepared to live that way! She stood at her loom and started weaving. Time seemed to pass more quickly. Before she realized it, it was midday. Elissa noticed that when you were not worrying, life could be pleasant and kind.

Agota, Elissa and Celandine sat at the table for lunch together. They chatted about their weaving, the stores, and the household. Celandine was interested in how they might redecorate the andron. She had some ideas for more impressive covers for the klines. Agota talked about the produce that was currently available in the market. As it was near the end of summer there was a lot of good food available at cheaper prices. Elissa listened happily.

Agota moved on to reminiscing about the past.

"I remember when you were a small girl, Elissa, you always used to go off to play at fighting wars with Zotikos," Agota said. "Later, when Timaios was old enough, you all used to go off together. You were like proper little hoplites! My little soldiers."

Elissa nodded. She thought about the times when the three of them used to play together. How she missed those Elysian days!

"Anyway," Agota continued, "you will be too busy in the future with your husband's household affairs and looking after your own children for that kind of play! You will have adult things on your mind. We all have to put our youths behind us."

Elissa nodded again.

After lunch, Elissa went back to her weaving. As she pushed the shuttle between the threads she started to feel something rising up within her. Some kind of terror, or rage, was thrusting up from her stomach and into her throat. She felt like she was going to scream. She left her loom and went downstairs to the courtyard.

Elissa sat on the low stone wall next to the water cistern and pondered what was happening to her. Everything was going so well, but when her mother started talking about the old days and the difficult adult life ahead her tranquil feelings evaporated! Suddenly the thought that she could never "play at war" with her brothers again threw her into the deepest, darkest despair. She felt afraid, desperate, overwhelmed. And there was hate and anger there too. This would never do. She had to find a way to get her thoughts back on track. She needed to find a path back to the wise resignation she had felt when she woke up that morning.

But no more play, no more fun in life! Just the duties of the household… almost being like a slave there herself! But why should she care about play? Was she still a child? No! Of course she wasn't. A woman must curb her wishes and attend to her duties – right? Of course this was right, as the Gods and the community had decreed.

Still, she did not feel convinced by these arguments. If it was not due to her being childish then what could be causing these doubts? Perhaps she was a bad person at heart. Or was there something else wrong with her? Maybe her mind was unsound. How could she know? She remembered that she had prayed to Athena for guidance at the household shrine, but she must not have received an answer as she still felt so restless. Maybe her offering had not been accepted. Or maybe the household shrine was not official enough. It might be better to go to the village altar.

Elissa went upstairs and asked her mother for permission to go to the village altar to Athena and pray there. Agota agreed and said that she would come with her to make some offerings of her own on behalf of the household. Elissa and Agota went to their bedrooms and changed into finer, colorfully-patterned peploses, and then proceeded to the storeroom to select some choice offerings for the altar: olive oil, olives, honey cakes and bread. They packed the offerings in a basket, put on their sandals and outdoor hats, and left the house to walk to the village altar.

Agota and Elissa approached the low entrance gate in the waist-high stone walls that surrounded the sacred area of Athena's altar. They removed their hats and then scooped up some water from the basin near the entrance, sprinkling it over their heads and bodies to purify themselves. The priestesses of Athena came forward and opened the gate, allowing Agota and Elissa to enter the sacred area, as they were the wife and daughter of Yorgos, a valued citizen of Oe. The priestesses took the offerings, prayed over them, and carried them to the open-air altar.

The altar was made of stone and marble, with Athena's name carved on the side. The priestesses placed the olives, honey cakes and bread on the marble top of the altar and prayed over them again. They also poured the olive oil on the altar and prayed over that. Agota stood near the altar, raised her hands toward the sky and prayed, asking Athena to grant health and prosperity to Yorgos's family and household.

While her mother was praying at the altar, Elissa also made her prayer, in silence. Inside her head, she asked Athena for guidance. "What is the right way to live? How could she know it for herself? Was there something wrong with her? Was she a bad person at heart? How could she know? What could she do about it? What would wisdom decree?"

As Elissa was praying she noticed a small marble statue of Athena out of the corner of her eye. For a moment she could have sworn it was smiling at her. Or was this just her imagination? She closed her eyes and returned to her prayers.

Agota had finished praying. She tapped on Elissa's shoulder, gesturing for her to follow. They thanked the priestesses and left the sacred area via the opening in the low wall. Agota had to check on some of the household orders, so they visited a few of the village stores on the way home.

As they walked home, Elissa thought about Athena. Did that small statue of the goddess really smile at her? If only there was some way of asking Athena, or the other Gods, directly. Then she would know the real answer of the truth!

They arrived home and went up to the gynaikon. Celandine was calmly weaving at her loom. Elissa and her mother returned to their work.

In the late afternoon, Elissa went to the courtyard to wait for her father to come home. As he entered the courtyard she called out to him: "Can I speak to you privately, Father?"

"Of course, Elissa," Yorgos replied. He took her into the empty andron. "What did you want to see me about?"

"I am troubled in my mind, Father," Elissa began. "I am worried about my character as a person. I am not sure if I am wicked or faulty. It seems to me that the only way to be sure is to ask the Gods directly. I can only know the truth about myself if I face them. I have tried making offerings and prayers, but I am not sure if I have been heard or not. I would like your permission to go to Mount Olympus and speak to the Gods directly."

Yorgos was stunned by this request. What was Elissa talking about? There was nothing wrong with her. Go to Mount Olympus! Surely there were simpler and better ways to get answers about the will of the Gods!

"This idea is ridiculous, Elissa!" Yorgos said. "It would be better to consult with the priests and wise men to get answers, not set out on a reckless and expensive journey to a faraway place. It may even be sacrilegious to go there!"

"But, Father…" Elissa began.

"No, Elissa," Yorgos interrupted. "I don't need to remind you that it is the duty of a young kore to listen to and obey her father's wishes. Put these concerns about yourself out of your head. You should be focusing on preparing yourself for your marriage, not going on crazy, pointless journeys.

You don't know what dangers you might face. I want you to stay home and prepare yourself for marriage. That is all I have to say on the matter."

Elissa stood and bowed humbly. She left the room and returned to the gynaikon. She did not say anything to her mother and sister about the conversation.

Later that night, as she lay on her bed, Elissa realized that she was never going to be satisfied until she found the answers to her questions for herself. There was nothing else for it: she was going to have to go to Mount Olympus and ask the Gods for their advice. She didn't want to disobey her father and upset her mother and sister, but she could not see any choice in the matter. How could she live with the doubts about her own character still clamoring in her head? How could she obey and make a good wife to some man if there were unanswered questions about her own suitability for this life? She just had to know! She would have to run away and make the journey by herself, no matter how dangerous it might be.

Elissa got up from her bed and started to collect her most valuable jewelry from her jewelry box. She had some gold and silver hair clips and pins decorated with gemstones and pearls. She also had ornamented clothes pins, several gold bracelets for her wrists and two for her upper arm – one had ends shaped into lions' heads. Elissa checked inside the box for the rest of her treasures. She took out jeweled gold rings and earrings, and a fine set of necklaces. The rings and earrings had stones of topaz, ruby, emerald, carnelian, agate, amethyst and garnet. Elissa carefully rolled the most expensive items in the folds of a cloth and tied it closed with some thread. She hoped she would be able to trade these for food and goods on the journey.

When all the household was asleep, Elissa crept downstairs to the storeroom and the kitchen. She took a piece of strong cloth and filled it with food and equipment. She gathered the ends of the cloth together, tied them with rope, and then quietly carried the bundle upstairs.

Back in her bedroom, Elissa added the roll of cloth containing her jewelry, what coins she had, and some sundry items, including a himation for the cold, to the bundle. She hid the bundle in her clothes chest and returned to bed. Soon she fell asleep and dreamt about her journey.

The next morning, Elissa got up and fetched a waxed wooden board from her table. She scratched a message on the waxed surface with a wooden stylus: "I am sorry that I had to do this to you all. I have to find the truth for myself. I will return home as soon as I have completed my quest. Please don't worry about me. Elissa." She put the board inside her chest and went to the gynaikon for breakfast.

Elissa ate quietly with her mother and sister. She helped with the tidying up after the meal and then stood at her loom and continued with her weaving. Later, she accompanied her mother to check the household and instruct the house slaves.

After lunch, Elissa asked her mother if she could go to the forest to practice her javelin throwing one last time. Agota was glad that Elissa was planning to turn away from her boyish pursuits and gave her permission to go.

Elissa went along the walkway and entered her room, closing the door behind her. She went to her chest and took out the waxed wooden board, propping it up on her pillow where it could be seen by anyone entering the room. She changed into a sturdy plain peplos and put on her strongest sandals. She returned to her chest and retrieved her travel bundle. She also grabbed her hunting javelin and then, after checking that no one was watching, went quietly downstairs to the courtyard. She bowed before the household statue of Athena and placed a small offering in front of it. She also made an offering to the household statue of Hermes that stood near the main entrance door. She checked that no one was in the andron and crept inside. She covered her hair and face with a veil, donned a wide-brimmed straw traveling hat, and discreetly exited via the andron's private door to the street.

With her travel bundle tied to her javelin and slung over her shoulder, Elissa walked silently through the village, crossed the fields, and joined the road to Delphi.

2. TERIS

"**H**ave you seen Elissa?" Agota asked Celandine. "She will be late for dinner."

"No, Mother. She has not come back from the forest yet," Celandine replied.

"Well, I don't know what could have happened to her. She is never late like this. I hope she hasn't encountered one of those wild boars again!" Agota said.

Agota started to worry. What if Elissa had run into another wild boar, but this time she had not been saved? Maybe her dear daughter was wounded out there, lying in the field, bleeding. What should she do? But, on the other hand, Elissa may be running late just because this was the last time she was going to practice her javelin-throwing skills.

She was going to change her ways and start the life that a good woman should lead. Yes, it was probably that: just a delay while she finished up her old youthful life.

Agota sat down to dinner with Celandine.

After they had eaten and the slaves had taken the dishes and cups away, Agota started wondering how long Elissa would be. It would soon be dark outside: not a good time for a young kore to be out on her own. She called for Dora.

"Dora, have you seen Elissa? Has she come home yet?" Agota asked.

"No, Mistress," Dora replied.

"Have any of the other slaves seen her?"

"I will check, Mistress," Dora replied.

Dora left and returned after a few minutes.

"No one has seen her come back, Mistress," Dora said.

Agota was worried now. This was not like Elissa. She dismissed Dora and got up from the table. She went to Elissa's room. Maybe her daughter had come home quietly and was resting there.

Elissa was not in the room. Her bed was still made up from the morning. No one had been lying there. Agota noticed the wooden board propped up on Elissa's pillow. She retrieved it and saw that there was writing scratched onto the waxed surface, but she could not read it. She would have to take it to Yorgos or one of the boys.

Agota left the room and went downstairs. She saw Zotikos in the courtyard.

"Zoti!" Agota called.

"Yes, Mother?" Zotikos replied.

"Could you read this, please?" Agota asked, handing him the waxed board.

"Yes, Mother. It says: 'I am sorry that I had to do this to you all. I have to find the truth for myself. I will return home as soon as I have completed my quest. Please don't worry about me. Elissa.' What has happened? Where has she gone?" Zotikos asked.

"Don't concern yourself with that for the moment," Agota replied. "First, I will talk to your father."

"Yes, Mother," Zotikos acknowledged.

"Yorgos! Where are you?" Agota called.

"In here!" Yorgos's voice came from the andron.

"May I see you?"

"Yes. Please come in," Yorgos invited.

The male slaves stood back from the doorway, allowing Agota to enter the room. Yorgos and Timaios were inside, discussing the events of the day while they waited for their evening meal. Yorgos got up from his kline and came over to Agota.

"What is it, dear?" Yorgos asked.

Agota handed him the board.

"I found this in Elissa's bedroom," Agota said. "She has not returned from javelin practice."

Yorgos took the board nearer to a window and read.

"Oh no," Yorgos muttered. "So, it has come to this!"

"What, dear?" asked Agota.

"Nothing," Yorgos replied. "I'm afraid that Elissa has gone off on a quest… on her own! Let me think about what to do. I'll take care of it."

"But will she be all right?" Agota asked, concerned. "Where has she gone? How can she go on her own? Is it far?"

"No, no, it's okay," Yorgos comforted. "I know where she has gone. She couldn't have got far. We should be able to bring her back. Leave it with me and I will organize things."

"Very well, dear," Agota replied.

"Yes. Just go upstairs and leave it with me and the boys," Yorgos said.

Agota nodded and returned to the gynaikon.

Yorgos asked Zotikos and Timaios to go to the kitchen and have their evening meal there. He then sat on the edge of a kline and thought. In spite of his command not to go, Elissa had run off to Mount Olympus on her own! She really was a headstrong young woman! But she couldn't have realized just how dangerous such a journey might be. Not even a fit young warrior would attempt a journey like that on his own! He would have to do something to bring her back. But what?

Yorgos considered getting a party together from the village and racing up into the mountains to find Elissa and bring her home, but if he did that then the whole village would know what had happened. Elissa's reputation would be ruined. How would he find a good-quality husband for her after she had done a thing like this? What reputable family would trust their son with a woman who might disobey him and run away at any moment? Nobody would want her. She would be doomed to stay in her father's home for the rest of her life: a shamed woman.

What about the rest of his family's reputation? What would the village leaders say about him and his family after a thing like this had happened? They would think that he had raised a willful daughter, that he did not know how to discipline her! They would question the morals of her mother, Agota. They would wonder if the other daughter, Celandine, was also tainted by this impetuous, disobedient spirit. In any case, no one of merit could associate themselves with such a family. This could have significant financial implications for Yorgos and his household. Would decent citizens want to trade with him anymore? Might they not think that it was "too sordid" to deal with him after this?

Yorgos knew that he might be exaggerating the impact of Elissa's actions, but he felt it was better to err on the side of caution. Better to do what was safest for everyone in this matter. But, then, what would happen to Elissa? He couldn't just leave her to her fate. What could he do to protect her?

As Yorgos sat wondering what to do, finding no satisfactory answer, there was a knock on the door to the andron.

"Yes? Who is it?" Yorgos asked.

"There is a man here to see you," a slave replied.

"Show him in," Yorgos commanded.

The door opened and a young man walked in. He had an athletic build and looked like he had dressed for hunting or adventure. He wore a dark green chiton and had a leather-sheathed kopis slung from his belt. On his back was a pack stuffed full with supplies. He had dark curly hair, and his equally dark eyes gazed calmly at Yorgos. He bowed.

"I am Teris, son of Herodotos, sir," the young man announced softly. "With respect, I have come to help you."

"You have?" Yorgos replied. "But in regard to what… sorry, I am forgetting myself. I know your father, he is a respected citizen and friend of mine. Welcome, Teris."

Teris bowed again.

"Please, would you care for some wine?" Yorgos invited.

"Thank you, but no, sir," Teris replied. "I think that the matter is too urgent for pleasantries, with respect."

"What matter is that?" Yorgos said, gesturing for Teris to sit on one of the klines.

Teris accepted the invitation and sat near Yorgos.

"Sir, I know that Elissa has run away," Teris began. "With your permission, I would like to protect her on her journey."

"But how did you know!" Yorgos exclaimed.

Teris smiled quietly in reply.

"Okay: you know," Yorgos conceded. "Can you bring her back?"

While he was talking, Yorgos was also thinking. This Teris was one of Elissa's prospective husbands. Yorgos had been speaking to his father, Herodotus, about it, but he had never spoken to Teris directly on the matter. Nothing had been decided yet. It was a fine family, but could he trust Teris with Elissa? In any case, he wanted Elissa brought home… and without dishonor to the family name!

"I may be able to, sir," replied Teris.

"And what will be the price?" asked Yorgos. "Do you want gold? Or money? I am willing to pay. Or is it something else that you want?"

Teris looked calmly at Yorgos.

"I do not want anything in return," Teris said.

"Maybe, maybe," said Yorgos. "Or maybe you want Elissa's hand in marriage?"

"Sir, I do not want any commitment from you. I only seek your permission to try to protect Elissa from harm," Teris replied.

"That is a very noble answer!" Yorgos said admiringly. "You certainly seem to be a fine young man." He stopped to consider. "Could you bring Elissa home? That would be the safest and best solution for us all."

"Sir, I could try. But if I should fail and she chooses to continue on her journey, will you allow me to go with her and try to protect her, to the best of my ability?" Teris replied.

Yorgos considered.

"Very well, young man," Yorgos said. "Try to bring her home. But if you can't convince her then I give you my blessing to try to protect her as best as you can."

Teris stood.

"Thank you, sir. I will depart now as time is short," Teris said. He strode to the doorway.

"My prayers go with you for your success," said Yorgos, also standing. "And, please, keep all this to yourself, you understand?"

Teris nodded and left.

After Teris had departed, Yorgos sat in the andron, worrying. What if young Teris could not convince Elissa to come home? He knew how headstrong his daughter could be! Would Teris be able to protect her on his own? He was just one young man! Who knows what dangers they may face out there on that long journey to the realm of the Gods? But he decided to keep all these fears to himself. It would be better if his family did not know the doubts that were lurking in his mind.

Elissa was climbing the dry dusty road to Delphi in the hills above Oe. The sun was nearing the horizon. Soon it would be dusk. In the distance, she could see some men coming the other way. As they got closer she saw that they looked a bit scruffy. Their chitons were worn and had not been washed for some time. She thought that it would be best to ignore them and pass by on the other side of the road.

The men had been watching Elissa approach and they decided to block her way. She looked a tasty young thing, with her long dark hair, spotless peplos and simple cloth bundle hanging from the javelin slung over her shoulder.

"What are you doing out here, young miss?" one of the men asked, winking lasciviously.

"So late in the evening," the second man added, giving a lewd stare.

The third man stood right in front of her, blocking her way with outstretched arms. There was no room for Elissa to get past. Elissa thought that she had better talk her way out of this, but she didn't have any experience of dealing with rude fellows. In Oe, as the daughter of Yorgos, everyone treated her with respect. But here on the road what status did she have?

"Please let me pass, citizens," Elissa tried.

The men laughed.

"Please let me pass," they repeated in a mocking tone.

A young man suddenly emerged from the bushes and stepped onto the road. He was athletic and wore a dark green chiton. He was carrying a double-ended spear and wore a leather-sheathed kopis on his belt.

"What is happening here, citizens?" the young man asked.

The rough men sized him up. He didn't look old enough to be much of a threat to the three of them.

"Mind your own business, lad, and get lost," the first one instructed.

The young man did not move. He stood calmly on the road.

"Leave my friend alone and continue with your journey," the young man advised.

The men laughed.

"You leave your 'friend' to us and *you* continue with *your* journey," the first one replied.

Teris suddenly moved forward and the first man was lying on his back on the dusty road. A puff of dry dust rose into the air from the impact. His two friends observed the action and decided it would be wiser to keep walking. They resumed their journey toward Oe. They did not look back.

Teris offered his hand to the man lying on the road. The man shook his head and stood up by himself.

"Tell your girlfriend to be more careful about who she encourages in future," he said gruffly. Then he turned and followed his companions.

Teris watched him go, without comment. He turned to Elissa.

"Are you all right?" Teris asked.

Elissa nodded. She was feeling a little foolish.

"I am Teris. I have seen you in Oe, Elissa, daughter of Yorgos," Teris said.

Elissa examined Teris. He had dark curly hair and very dark eyes, made even darker by the failing light of the evening. He appeared to be some kind of hunter, in his somber green chiton, but his double-ended spear was that of a hoplite. He certainly looked athletic enough to be a warrior! Not too hard on the eyes, Elissa thought, but she had more important things to focus on at the moment.

"I do not know you, Teris, but I am glad that you came along at this exact moment!"

Teris bowed.

"I have to put a question to you," Teris said. "I have come from your father, Yorgos, and I must ask if you would be prepared to return to your home with me."

"I thank you, Teris, for your kind help, but I must continue on my journey," Elissa replied.

"I see," said Teris. "In that case, may I request your permission to accompany you? Perhaps I could be of service to you."

Elissa had mixed feelings. She felt glad that she would have the company, help, and possible protection of this young man. But, at the same time, she had expected to travel alone, and especially not with a man, on her quest.

"You may come with me if you wish. But I must ask that if you do decide to come you will give your commitment to not interfere with my plan to go to Mount Olympus," Elissa said.

"I give you my commitment," Teris replied gravely.

"Thank you. Then let us proceed!" Elissa said.

Teris suggested that as it was getting dark it would be a good time to set up camp for the night. They left the road and found a suitable site. Teris collected wood and started a small fire with his flint and steel. Elissa and Teris shared some of their supplies for dinner: fresh bread, cheese, olives and apples.

The next day, Elissa and Teris continued on the road to Delphi. It was little more than a track. At first the path was dry and dusty, with only a few shrubs and olive trees around, but as they climbed they entered the forested hills. In the forest they were able to supplement their supplies by catching a few hares. Elissa's skill with her hunting javelin proved very useful here! Teris helped with his multipurpose kopis, preparing the hares for roasting over the fire.

Over the next few days they passed a few travelers going each way on the track. Some had gone to Delphi to consult the Oracle and were returning home to Athens. Others had gone on the pilgrimage just to make offerings and pray to Apollo, as they could not afford the high expense of the Oracle. Being young and not carrying much, Elissa and Teris overtook the slower travelers going toward Delphi, but sometimes they met them again after they had taken time off to hunt for game and cook their meals in the forest.

On the afternoon of the third day, the forest started to thin out as the track descended to some grassy plains that were surrounded by hills. Elissa and Teris decided to make camp away from the track, near the Asopos River. After they had collected wood for the fire, Elissa took the opportunity to go down to the river to wash off the road grime. Teris stayed at the campsite, tending the fire.

A satyr was sitting near the river. He saw Elissa approaching and crouched down among the bushes so he could not be seen. He watched Elissa carefully. Elissa took off her sandals and waded into the fresh-smelling water. She started to wash herself and her clothes. The satyr liked what he saw. What a tasty young woman! He stood up and stepped out from the bushes.

Elissa saw the strange creature emerge and walk toward her on his hairy, hooved legs. He had a man's upper body, but he looked like a goat from the waist down. His face was bearded; two goat horns protruded from his head.

Elissa felt afraid of the strange creature, but thought that it would be better to hide her feelings.

"Hello," Elissa said. "It is a pleasant evening. What do you want?"

"I want a good time!" the satyr replied.

Elissa waded to the edge of the river and climbed onto the bank. She wrung some of the water out of the peplos she was still wearing, then picked up her sandals and walked over to the satyr, smiling.

"That sounds like a great idea," Elissa said. "Everyone loves a good time."

The satyr nodded enthusiastically.

"Wine helps people to have a good time," Elissa declared. "What do you think?"

The satyr smiled. "You are so right, there! Wine is from the Gods."

"I think Dionysus would agree with you!" laughed Elissa.

"Yes, yes!" replied the satyr, eagerly.

"Then let us return to my campsite to get it!" suggested Elissa.

"Lead on, young lady!" the satyr said, bowing.

Elissa put on her sandals and proceeded toward the campsite. The satyr followed her happily.

"Do you live around here?" Elissa asked as they walked.

"Yes. We all live around here… near the water and in the forest," the satyr replied. "Me and my friends."

"How is that?" asked Elissa.

"We are always having a good time. We do as Dionysus would want... and Pan. But sometimes we run out of wine, which is a great shame!" the satyr joked.

"That can't be much fun," Elissa agreed. "We will be able to remedy that soon!"

Elissa and the satyr approached the small fire burning at the campsite. Teris saw them and started to draw his kopis from its leather sheath.

"There's no need for that, Teris," Elissa said. "We only came for a drink."

The satyr smiled and nodded at Teris congenially.

Teris quietly pushed his kopis back into its sheath.

Elissa walked over to her travel bundle and took out a wineskin. She removed the cork, drank a little, and then offered it to the satyr. The satyr grabbed it and gulped down some wine. Teris watched him.

"Let's have some music," Elissa said. She started singing.

The satyr stopped drinking and lifted his pan-pipes, which were hanging from a strap slung around his neck, and accompanied Elissa. He danced around the fire as he played. From time to time, he took a few more swigs from the wineskin.

Teris did not join the festivities. He sat quietly by the fire and watched the events through hooded eyes. His sheathed kopis lay on the ground beside him.

Elissa moved from song to song while the satyr played his pipes and drank. The satyr stared at

Elissa, scanning her young fit body with hungry eyes. Elissa just smiled and kept singing.

The satyr was quite drunk now. He stopped playing and lay down by the fire. Elissa ceased her singing and sat down too, but well out of reach of the satyr.

Teris looked at the satyr in the firelight.

"You know, you might be able to have some fun," Teris said.

The satyr lifted his horned head and peered drowsily across at Teris.

"Surely you know some forest nymphs?" Teris asked.

The satyr nodded.

"Imagine searching them out and having some fun with them," Teris suggested.

"That's a good idea," the satyr replied. He licked his lips.

Teris collected some of their food supplies and extracted a new wineskin from his pack. He offered them to the satyr.

"Take these," Teris said. "You will be able to share them with the nymphs you find and have a good time together!"

The satyr took the offerings and staggered away, drunkenly singing to himself as he went.

Elissa watched him go.

"That was a close one," Elissa observed.

Teris nodded.

"You handled him well," Teris said.

"Thank you. Quite an adventure," Elissa replied. "I don't think he meant any harm."

Teris nodded slowly but didn't speak.

"Is there anything to eat? After all that excitement, I'm famished," said Elissa.

Teris nodded and took out a hare. He prepared it and roasted it on the fire. The two ate their meal and then got some sleep. But from time to time, Teris woke and looked around himself, his kopis and spear ready by his side.

The next morning, Elissa and Teris broke camp and continued on their journey. They crossed grassy plains for days and then ascended into the mountains. Here, the grass gave way to forested areas of oak, Greek strawberry, bay laurel, cedar, and other trees. The air was slightly cooler, but it still got hot in the middle of the day. The shade afforded by the trees and the occasional sprinkle of rain were very welcome.

As they continued on the trail, they encountered an increasing number of fellow travelers heading to and from Delphi. After two days of traveling in the mountains, they arrived at a clearing. Many people were there, bustling up and down. Buildings came into view. There were places to stay, shops, and market stalls. Elissa and Teris took the opportunity to trade some of their valuables in return for more supplies. Elissa bought a good-quality goat to offer to Apollo. Teris bought a new wineskin to replace the one he had given to the satyr. Teris also bought a pack for Elissa, similar to the one he wore. He told Elissa that it should make it easier for her to carry her belongings. Elissa thanked him for the thoughtful gift.

After completing their trading, Elissa and Teris proceeded along the road to the Sanctuary of Athena Pronaia. They tethered the goat outside and entered the complex. At the altar they made some offerings to Athena Pronaia. Elissa prayed for Athena's help on her quest and thanked her for her support thus far. Elissa and Teris then left the sanctuary complex and continued on the road. They passed the gymnasium, where athletes trained for the Pythian Games, held every four years at the Delphi stadium. Further along the road they came across the Castalian Spring. They stopped to purify themselves by washing there and drinking the sacred water. Finally, they arrived at the Sanctuary of Apollo complex. The complex was located on a steep mountain slope and was surrounded by stone walls. Terraces were cut into the slope to support the various magnificent buildings. Some priests stopped them at the entrance gate and asked them their business. Teris explained that they had come to make offerings to Apollo and consult the Oracle. The priests inspected the goat and told them that they were lucky as the Pythia only consulted on the seventh day of the month, which happened to be today! Teris and Elissa thanked them and were allowed to enter the complex after first washing their hands in the sacred water kept in basins near the entrance.

The pair walked along the wide paved path, known as the Sacred Way. On either side of them were numerous impressive statues and buildings.

They passed a large bronze statue of a bull on the right and then a group of thirteen bronze statues on the left. In the center of the thirteen was a statue of the Athenian general, Miltiades, who had led the Hellenes to victory over the Persian invaders at Marathon. Miltiades stood between statues of the gods of Athens and Delphi: Athena and Apollo. The ten other statues were of Attican heroes. At the base of the statues was a dedication reading: "The Athenians to Apollo from the Persians as best spoils of the battle in Marathon." After these were more statues on a semicircular pedestal on the left, then some on a long pedestal erected by the Spartan colony of Taras. An open-sided treasury building followed. After this was an opulent, fully enclosed treasury building, made entirely of marble. The entrance had two inner columns in the form of female statues holding up the architrave. The front frieze and pediment featured brightly painted, sculpted scenes of the Battle of Troy, with the Gods arguing on behalf of each side, and of Heracles attempting to steal the oracular tripod of Apollo, with Zeus intervening. On the side of the treasury there was a longer frieze showing the ancient battle between the Gods and the Titans. Elissa and Teris could only imagine what rich votive offerings to Apollo were locked inside.

Elissa and Teris arrived at a turning in the Sacred Way, the stepped path leading up and to the right. They passed further treasury buildings which were less opulent than the marble one below, most being constructed of gray limestone blocks. On the left they saw a more stylish treasury building which had two Doric columns on the inner side of the entrance. The whole structure was made of marble. There were beautiful painted sculptures in the entry area and sculpted scenes from the adventures of Heracles and Theseus wrapped around all four sides of the building near the roofline. Multiple inscriptions were carved on the base of the treasury's platform. Elissa found one saying: "The Athenians dedicated this to Apollo as first fruits from the Persians at the Battle of Marathon." Another Athenian triumph, she thought.

Looking upward in the direction of the temple of Apollo, Elissa could see a tall column with a giant marble sphinx on top. The sphinx, with its head of a woman, breast and wings of a bird, and lower body of a lion, watched over the scene below, tirelessly guarding the temple day and night.

Elissa and Teris continued along the Sacred Way until they reached a turning to the left and upward. From here they could see a huge statue of Apollo towering over the complex. They climbed the sloping, stepped path toward the altar. On the right they saw an enormous, 26-foot-high, bronze column made in the shape of three intertwined serpents. At the top of the column, the serpents' heads supported a golden tripod which had a golden bowl resting on it. Elissa wanted to check what this was for, but they were short of time. They had arrived at the altar to Apollo, which stood before his temple.

The priests came forward to greet them.

"Welcome to the Temple of Apollo," the priests said. They examined the goat and were satisfied with its quality. "We can make the sacrifice of the animal and check the entrails to see if the Pythia will see you today," they proposed.

"Thank you," said Elissa, and handed the priests some of her fine jeweled necklaces as an offering.

The priests accepted the necklaces and led the goat to the white and black marble altar. Other worshippers, who were also waiting to see the Pythia, watched as the goat was slaughtered and its entrails were carefully examined. The priests seemed happy with what they saw. They came over to Elissa and Teris.

"The signs are good," the lead priest said. "We will arrange for you to see the Pythia. It will take some time, but if you would care to wait with the others we will come and get you when she is available."

"Thank you," Elissa replied.

"No, not you," the lead priest said. "Women are not allowed into the temple. We will collect the young man…?" he trailed off, looking at Teris.

"Teris," Teris replied.

"Teris. Thank you. We will collect you as soon as possible," the lead priest advised.

The priests went into the temple.

"Sorry, Elissa," Teris said.

"That's okay," Elissa replied. "I should have expected this. Women are never allowed into a male God's temple."

"But the Pythia is a woman, isn't she?" Teris objected.

"That's different," Elissa responded.

"What do you want me to ask her?" Teris inquired.

"Oh. Okay," Elissa said. She thought for a moment. "Could you ask her for guidance on my journey? Should I be making this journey to Mount Olympus or not? What does Apollo think? I do not want to offend anyone."

Teris looked thoughtful. He nodded. "Yes, I can do that," he replied.

Elissa turned and watched what was happening at the altar. Her sacrificial goat was being cut up by the priests. They placed some of the pieces on the white marble top of the altar and took the more edible parts into the temple.

Elissa quickly tired of watching the activities at the altar and turned her attention to the temple of Apollo. The front faced her. It was made of poros stone with white Parian marble pediments. Elissa could see six pillars in the Doric style with a colorfully-painted frieze on the pediment above. It showed Apollo's chariot being pulled by his four horses as he arrived at Delphi from Athens. Elissa moved closer to study the frieze. To the right of Apollo's chariot were three men, one was welcoming Apollo. To the left of the chariot were three young women. Elissa wondered who they all were. On each side of the scene were two lions. The one on the left side was attacking a bull; the one on the right was attacking a stag. Elissa hoped that she wouldn't have to meet any lions on her journey!

Elissa moved closer to the temple entrance, but some priests stepped in front of her and gestured for her to go back.

"Men only," the priests said.

Elissa turned to Teris. "Could you get a closer look?"

Teris frowned. "I am not sure if it is appropriate," he replied. "I will wait to see if I am permitted to enter and then look."

"Okay. Suit yourself," Elissa replied casually.

Teris nodded seriously.

They went back to the waiting area near the altar.

"What do you intend to do if the Pythia says you should not go on to Mount Olympus?" Teris asked in a low voice.

"I could not disobey the Gods," Elissa replied. "If Apollo says that I should not go then I will have to obey that."

Teris nodded.

"But that may not happen!" Elissa continued. "Maybe Apollo will tell the Pythia that I must go on!"

Teris gestured to Elissa to lower her voice. There were many people around them.

"Okay," Elissa said more quietly. "Let's just wait and see what the Pythia says about our journey."

"*Your* journey," Teris corrected. "But I will come with you to help you."

"Thank you for that," Elissa bowed.

While they waited, the people who had arrived before them were taken in turn into the temple by the priests. Eventually, it was Teris's turn. He said goodbye to Elissa and followed the priests up the ramp that led into the temple.

The forecourt of the temple had sayings written on the upper area of the wall. Above the doorway was written: "Know Thyself." Teris made a mental note of this so he could think about it later. On the upper left side of the wall was written: "Nothing Too Much," and on the upper right side was: "In a Pledge Ruin is Present." Teris also took note of these for later.

The priests led Teris through the open doorway into the main chamber of the temple. The room was filled with beautiful statues of the Gods. The most striking was a gold statue of Apollo. There was also an altar to Poseidon, the God of the sea. The group continued to the back of the main chamber, where there was an opening to a second, smaller room. A few steps led down into the room. The Pythia, dressed in a plain white peplos, was waiting inside. At the back of the room was a small curtained recess. The priests ushered Teris into the recess and closed the curtains behind them.

"What is your question?" the lead priest asked Teris.

"I would like to know if my friend, Elissa, daughter of Yorgos of Attica, should continue on her quest to go to Mount Olympus to consult the Gods," Teris answered.

The priests looked a little startled, but quickly regained their composure.

"We have received your question, Teris. Is there anything else you would like to ask?" the lead priest said.

"No, that is all," Teris replied.

"Very well. We will consult the Pythia," the lead priest said. "Wait here."

Teris sat on a cool marble bench that was the only furniture in the recess. The priests left the waiting area, closing the curtains behind them, and went over to the Pythia. The lead priest told the Pythia the question for Apollo.

The Pythia walked over to a brass tripod, whose legs straddled a chasm in the rock floor of this part of the temple. She climbed into the bowl-shaped seat of the tripod and waited for the sweet-smelling gases that came up from the chasm to reach her. She breathed deeply, inhaling the vapors, entering into a trance. She began to twitch convulsively and sounds emerged from her lips. Teris could hear them from behind the curtains, but he could not make any sense out of what he heard. The priests watched and listened carefully. After a short time the Pythia stopped twitching and became silent. She tiredly climbed down from the tripod and went outside to rest.

The priests opened the curtains and gestured for Teris to follow them. The priests led Teris out of the temple and asked him to wait in the forecourt for their findings. While he waited, Teris studied the sayings written on the forecourt wall again. "Know Thyself" seemed like very good advice. A person should know themselves before they set out to do something. That way they would know what they could achieve and what they could not.

The priests interrupted Teris's musings.

"We have interpreted the message from Apollo," the lead priest said.

Teris nodded expectantly.

"Yes. The message was not meaningful," the lead priest continued. "We believe that this signifies that Apollo has no answer for you today."

Teris felt disappointed. What was he going to tell Elissa?

"I see. Please thank the Pythia for her efforts," Teris said.

The priests nodded and departed. Teris took a moment to collect his thoughts. They had come all this way and Elissa had spent so much to be told this! "No answer for you today." Teris felt sad for Elissa. How would she take this? There was nothing else to do now but go and tell her. He left the forecourt and went in search of his traveling companion.

Elissa was admiring the huge statue of Apollo that stood near the waiting area. She stared up at the giant representation of the God. He was holding the figurehead from the front of a naval ship in his hand. Elissa looked at the pedestal supporting the statue. There was an inscription carved into the stone, reading: "The Hellenes dedicated this to Apollo from the Persian spoils of the Battle of Salamis." Elissa remembered that this was the famous naval defeat of the invading Persians by an outnumbered Hellenic fleet of triremes. The Hellenic triremes had rammed and sunk the Persian ones, thanks to heroic effort and clever strategy. It was this battle that turned the tide of the Persian invasion and allowed the Hellenic states to remain free.

Teris had seen Elissa and came up to her.

"That was for Salamis," he commented, gazing up at the statue.

"Yes," Elissa replied. "Did the Pythia see you? What did she say?"

Teris frowned. "Yes, she saw me. But she did not have much to say."

"What happened?" Elissa asked, feeling dismayed.

"I was shown into the temple and I had to stay behind a curtain in a waiting area. I could hear the Pythia making strange noises. Then, after a while, the priests came and told me that these meant that Apollo had no answer for us today," Teris replied.

"No answer?" Elissa said. "What could that mean? You asked her about the quest?"

Teris nodded.

"Okay. So… Apollo had nothing to say about our journey to Mount Olympus," Elissa mused.

"Will you be going home then?" Teris asked.

"Going home? Why should I do that?" Elissa replied. "The Pythia did not say that I should return home."

"But she did not say anything… at least, according to the priests," Teris observed.

Elissa looked around. She noticed that some of the people nearby seemed to be listening in on their conversation.

"Let's get away from here," Elissa suggested.

Teris nodded and they moved away from the waiting area. They went a short distance down the Sacred Way. Elissa spotted a stoa which backed onto the retaining wall below the Temple of Apollo.

"Let's go over there," Elissa pointed.

The two left the Sacred Way and walked over to the stoa. There were seven marble columns at the front of the stoa. A wooden roof ran back from the columns to the retaining wall of the temple's terrace. Inside, Elissa and Teris could see parts of naval ships: ropes and prow figureheads. They entered the structure. It was cooler inside, thanks to the shade of the roof.

Elissa looked around and, not seeing anyone nearby, continued the conversation.

"Teris, Apollo did not say anything… or… he did say something!" Elissa exclaimed.

"What did he say?" Teris asked. "I am not sure that I understand you."

"Didn't the Pythia make some sounds?" Elissa asked.

"Yes," Teris replied.

"Then maybe Apollo *was* speaking through her," Elissa suggested.

"Saying what?"

"Maybe, maybe Apollo was saying that he doesn't want to tell us anything!" Elissa replied.

Teris looked thoughtful.

"Maybe he meant that it was up to us, not to the Gods, to say," Elissa continued. "What do you think?"

"It's possible," Teris said slowly. "Yes, it could be that."

"If I am right then we can continue. The Gods would not be against it," Elissa proposed.

"They may not be," Teris said.

"May not be," Elissa echoed. "You are right. They may be against me going. How would I know? Perhaps if I go to Mount Olympus I will be disobeying their will after all. Maybe I had better just go home then." She sank to the floor of the stoa.

"Perhaps I could be of some assistance?" a voice said, appearing to come from the air.

A man stepped out from behind one of the columns and came forward. He looked middle-aged, with some gray flecks in his dark hair and more in his long beard. He was thin and tall, and wore a full-length chiton with a himation wrapped over it as if the day was cold.

"I am sorry, I couldn't help but overhear you earlier. I am Smeme," the man said. "I have some experience of these matters and might be able to advise you."

Elissa stood and studied Smeme carefully. He seemed harmless enough. Maybe this stranger could help.

"I am Elissa, daughter of Yorgos of Oe, and this is Teris, son of Herodotos, also of Oe," Elissa said.

"Pleased to meet you," Smeme bowed.

Elissa bowed back, but Teris remained stiffly upright.

"Maybe we could sit over here?" Smeme suggested, pointing to some stone benches.

The three sat on the benches, facing each other.

"I have experience of the Gods and the prophecies of Apollo," Smeme began. "The thing to remember about Apollo is that he is also known as Loxias, which means ambiguous. He has, of course, the best of virtues, especially in art, music, poetry, beauty, health and behavior, but he can be a little tricky to understand. When he says something through the Pythia it has to be interpreted carefully."

"But he didn't say anything," Teris objected.

"You may think so," Smeme smiled, "but didn't the Pythia move and make sounds?"

"I couldn't tell if she moved," Teris replied, "but I did hear her making sounds."

"Precisely!" Smeme cried. "That means that Apollo was talking through her. Now, the priests have to interpret her movements and sounds to work out what Apollo meant. See? Then they tell that to you."

Teris nodded.

"And what did they tell you?"

"They said: 'We believe that this signifies that Apollo has no answer for you today,'" Teris recalled.

"We believe that this signifies!" Smeme whooped, slapping his thigh. "You see! They were not sure."

"Yes, I see," Teris nodded.

"Then what really happened? What did it mean?" Elissa demanded.

"My guess is that Apollo wanted you to know that the decision was yours. The Gods did not want to intervene today," Smeme proposed.

"Okay. Then should I go to Mount Olympus or not?" Elissa asked.

Smeme considered. "Isn't that up to you?" he said.

"But I don't want to do something that is not right," Elissa replied.

Smeme looked impressed. "You are correct to say that," he commended. "The Gods should not be mocked… or disregarded!"

Teris watched Smeme carefully.

Elissa thought. "Maybe since the Gods did not say I could not go, then I can go," Elissa said.

Smeme nodded.

"Okay. Then I will go! What do you think, Teris?" Elissa asked.

"I will come with you," Teris answered.

Elissa and Teris stood up.

"May I come with you, too?" Smeme asked, also standing.

"Why?" Teris demanded.

"I have been to many places, but I have never been to Mount Olympus," Smeme replied. "I would like to see it."

Teris looked unconvinced.

"And I may be of some use to you, my lady," Smeme bowed to Elissa.

Elissa was not sure that she wanted a third member in her party. But Smeme had been helpful to her. Perhaps his knowledge of the ways of the Gods would be useful to have around.

"What do you think, Teris? Would it be okay?" Elissa asked.

Teris frowned. "I think that is up to you, Elissa. This is your quest," he said.

"But I value your opinion," Elissa entreated.

Teris thought. "Okay, he can come," he answered.

"Thank you, Teris. You will be welcome on our journey, Smeme," Elissa said.

Smeme bowed. "Thank you, both," he said. "If we can stop by the inn on the way out of Delphi, I will collect my belongings."

"Of course," said Elissa. "We will be going via the town, too."

The three left the stoa and walked down the Sacred Way and out of the Sanctuary of Apollo.

3. SMEME

After Smeme had collected his belongings from the inn, most of which he carried in a backpack, the group left Delphi and took the narrow track that wound over the mountains to the north. The track got steeper and steeper and narrower and narrower. Eventually it started to level out near the top of the mountains. The travelers found themselves crossing between the peaks, with steep rocky slopes on either side of them. They came to a pass and started to go across, but a large Sphinx appeared in front of them, blocking the path. There were only two choices: go up to the Sphinx or turn and go back home. The team walked up to the Sphinx.

The Sphinx, with her lion's body, bird's wings and human female head, stared down at the little people as they cautiously approached.

"Excuse me, madam, would we be allowed to pass?" Elissa asked the Sphinx.

The Sphinx stared enigmatically at Elissa.

"You may pass, but only if you answer my riddle. If you fail, I will eat you," the Sphinx replied. "You can go back now or stay and be eaten."

Elissa turned to the others. "We must go on," she said.

"I agree, young lady," Smeme replied. "We must go on."

"I think it would be better to take the Sphinx's offer and return home," Teris said. "I wouldn't want anything to happen to you."

"Don't worry about me," Elissa replied. "You can go back if you wish. I won't think any the less of you."

Smeme watched the pair.

Teris shook his head.

"No, if you want to go on then I will stay with you," Teris stated.

The three turned to face the Sphinx.

"Ask your riddle," they said together.

The Sphinx smiled. "Very well. You look tasty enough. My riddle is: 'What is always in front of you but cannot be seen?'"

Elissa looked at Teris. "Is it around the corner?" she asked in a low voice.

"It cannot be that because a corner is not always in front of you," Teris murmured. "It must be what is right in front of you, but you cannot see it."

"Which is what?" Elissa said, looking puzzled. "Is it your nose? No. Then what? The air? That must be it," Elissa concluded, and turned to tell the Sphinx.

Smeme held up his hand, stopping Elissa.

"That is not the answer," Smeme said, "because sometimes you see the air, as happens when it is cold and turns to fog."

Elissa and Teris agreed.

"Let me answer," Smeme proposed. "I have had a little experience of these things in my travels."

"Okay," Elissa and Teris consented.

Smeme turned to face the Sphinx, which watched him hungrily.

"It is the future," Smeme answered.

The Sphinx looked disappointed.

"The future is always in front of you but it cannot be seen," Smeme added.

"You have answered correctly," said the Sphinx. "You may pass." It moved back and stood aside.

Smeme bowed to the Sphinx and waved Elissa and Teris through. The group gingerly squeezed past the Sphinx and walked a short distance down the path.

"Oh, Sphinx!" Smeme said, turning back to face the creature. "I have a riddle for you."

"For me!" the Sphinx exclaimed. "And if I do not answer you, little man, shall you eat me!" it smiled.

"No, you misunderstand me," Smeme replied. "I am so grateful to you for giving us a chance to pass that I would like to offer a riddle to you."

"Offer me a riddle? But I have many riddles!" the Sphinx boasted.

"Of course you do, Ancient One," Smeme replied. "But surely another couldn't hurt?"

The Sphinx considered. "Very well. Tell me your riddle, Hellene," it commanded.

"What goes away as soon as you name it?" Smeme replied.

"I know that one," the Sphinx said. "It is silence."

"You are right, oh great Sphinx," Smeme said admiringly. "Then do you know this one? What goes up but never comes down?"

The Sphinx pondered. "Is it smoke?" it asked.

"It could be," said Smeme, "but sometimes smoke comes down as ash."

"True," said the Sphinx. "Then what is the answer?"

"Age," Smeme replied.

"Age? That is very good!" said the Sphinx. "I will remember that one."

The Sphinx thought for a moment.

"I am very grateful to you," the Sphinx continued. "Since you have been so considerate and respectful toward me, I will give you something in return."

The Sphinx took out a bundle and offered it to Smeme.

"Take this cloak. It will protect you from harm by making you invisible," the Sphinx said.

Smeme stepped forward and took the bundled cloak. He put it into his backpack.

"Thank you, oh great and wonderful Sphinx!" Smeme said. He bowed to the Sphinx, but it had already turned back and was watching the pass again.

Smeme rejoined the others and the team continued on their way.

After they had been walking for a while and were well out of the sight and earshot of the Sphinx, Elissa thought it safe to speak.

"It sure was lucky that you came with us, Smeme!" Elissa observed. "I dread to think what would have happened if you hadn't been there!" She shuddered.

"I am glad to have been of some assistance," Smeme said, smiling and bowing.

"You know your way around Sphinxes!" Elissa applauded. "And their riddles!"

Smeme grinned in response.

Teris bowed to Smeme, but continued to watch him carefully. Despite his suspicions, he had to admit that Smeme really did know how to handle a Sphinx.

They walked a little further. The track widened now as it descended from the peaks. The party was able to walk abreast. Teris took the opportunity to question Smeme.

"How is that you know so much, Smeme?" Teris asked.

"I only know a thing or two, I'm afraid, Teris," Smeme replied. "I have traveled far and wide and for many years, as you can see by the lines on my face! I have seen some things and taken note of them," he added mysteriously.

Teris nodded thoughtfully.

"It must be wonderful to have traveled so far!" Elissa declared. "I wish that I, as a woman, could live a life like that!"

Smeme considered.

"Is it not a woman's lot to find a husband and live with him?" Smeme asked, secretly watching Teris.

"It is!" Elissa replied loudly. "But it is my quest to find out why," she continued. "Why is that what the Gods want… or is it what they want?"

Teris noticed that Smeme was watching him and looked away. Smeme nodded to himself and turned back to Elissa.

"Young lady," Smeme said, "I absolutely agree with you! That is why I am helping you on your quest… to the best of my humble abilities."

"And you have a goal of your own, too, don't you?" Teris interjected.

"I do. Yes. Thank you, young man," Smeme replied. "As do others in the party. Am I right?"

"You are, sir," Teris answered gruffly.

Elissa was concentrating on navigating along the rock-strewn path and did not seem to notice the exchange.

"So, where have you been?" Teris asked.

"Yes! Do tell us about your journeys!" Elissa urged.

"I have traveled far," Smeme replied. "I have been on the land and over the sea. I have crossed to islands. I have gone west and I have gone south. I have even seen Sparta."

"What was that like?" Elissa asked.

"It was an experience!" Smeme replied. "They are such tough people. The men train from childhood in the art of war. Actually, this will interest you, Elissa: the women of Sparta are much freer than those in the other city-states. They train in sports and are educated. They roam the city freely. They are called 'The mothers of our warriors' by the men. It seems that the Gods have a different view of their role there!"

"Is that so?" said Elissa. "That is amazing."

"It's not all good," said Smeme, "but for women it is a lot freer."

"But aren't Spartan men a bit rough?" Teris asked. "Is that true… what we have heard?"

"Yes, you could say that!" laughed Smeme. "Rough and tough! They have to be. Their upbringing is so harsh. Only the strongest survive."

"That is what I was told," Teris nodded.

"Where else have you been?" Elissa asked. "What were the people like there?"

"I have been to Corinth," Smeme replied. "The people there were fine. I have also been to Thebes – a proud people. And, of course, I have spent a lot of time in Athens. I think you know about the people there!"

"Why in Athens?" Elissa asked.

"Well, firstly, I was born there! But also, my favorite Goddess rules that city," Smeme replied.

"Athena?" queried Elissa.

"Yes, of course. The great and wise Athena," Smeme answered. "She has taught me much."

"What has Athena taught you?" Teris asked.

"This and that," replied Smeme. "Quite a few things of use in the world."

"I see," said Teris quietly.

"But I don't see!" complained Elissa. "What did she teach you?"

"I studied a bit," Smeme replied. "I know a few things."

"If you don't want to tell us just say so!" Elissa said angrily.

"It's hard to explain the things I know," Smeme replied calmly. "But they could be helpful on our journey."

"Okay!" Elissa snorted. "Have it your way." She moved ahead of the group and continued walking by herself.

Teris fell back and followed behind, keeping a close eye on Smeme.

The party continued walking through the mountains for a few days, resting at night. They were still heading north, climbing gradually, with some stretches of uphill and downhill terrain. The track wound through the mountains, surrounded by trees. Eventually, the track started to descend.

In Olympus, the Titan goddess of divine order, natural law and fairness, Themis, was hearing reports about Elissa. Spirits told her that Elissa had broken the natural order. She had left her good father's household without authorization and had started on a sacrilegious journey, of her own choosing, to Mount Olympus. There she planned to challenge the Gods to their holy faces.

This outrageous behavior could not be tolerated!

Themis held out her sword, which empowered her to cut fact from fiction, and summoned the Harpies. The Harpies, with their large birds' bodies and women's heads, soon arrived, screeching as they came. They flew down to the ground and stood on their sharply-taloned feet, ready for instruction.

"Go and find this human, Elissa, who has left Delphi and is on her way to Mount Olympus. She is to be brought for judgment for her transgression and arrogance against the natural order!" commanded Themis.

The Harpies leaped into the air, beating their huge wings, and flew off in search of Elissa. Themis could hear their outraged screeching as they sped toward the distant horizon.

Elissa and her party were continuing their descent down the mountain track when the Harpies found them. The Harpies dove shrieking upon Elissa. They were about to catch her in their talons when Teris jumped forward, waving his double-ended spear at them, blocking their way. The Harpies tried to get around him but the spear was always against them.

"What are you doing? Why are you here?" Teris shouted over the Harpies' angry screeching.

"We have to take this human for judgment!" the Harpies screamed. "She has broken the natural order."

"What natural order has she broken?" Teris demanded.

"That is not for us to say!" the Harpies shrieked. "Nor is it for you to question, puny human man. Hand her over at once or you will also be punished!"

"No!" Teris replied.

"Wait! Wait!" Smeme called. "I can assure you that Elissa, daughter of Yorgos of Oe, has not broken any natural order. I know her well, and her mission, and she and the mission are nothing but righteous."

The Harpies landed and stood facing the party.

"Stop talking and hand her over for judgment, Magos," the Harpies demanded.

"One moment, please," said Smeme. "I ask only for one moment before we hand her over. First, I need to think."

The Harpies stood watching, their dark eyes glaring.

Smeme raised his open hands toward the sky and began to pray.

"Dear Gods of Olympus, I beg for your indulgence," Smeme called. "Please send your poor servants guidance on the case of Elissa."

Smeme waited patiently, his arms still raised in the air.

A mist appeared on the side of the mountain and rolled toward them. A figure began to appear in the mist. It looked like Athena, holding a spear in her right hand and bearing a shield on the left. She was dressed in armor over her long peplos. On her head she wore a golden helmet crowned with an olive wreath. She stood tall above the party, looking down on them with stern gray eyes.

"Great and noble Athena, please tell us how Elissa, daughter of Yorgos of Oe, has offended the Gods and the natural order by undertaking her quest to go to Mount Olympus!" Smeme cried.

The giant spirit of the goddess considered, cold-faced. It looked down at the Harpies. It looked at Teris and then at Elissa. It turned its gaze back to the Harpies.

"Why are you here?" the spirit asked in a thunderous voice.

"We have been sent by Themis," the Harpies replied. "As the goddess of divine law and order, she cannot be questioned by any of the Gods," they asserted.

"Wait here for my return," the spirit commanded.

The Harpies flew to a nearby clearing and waited there. Teris kept his spear pointed in their direction, ready for any trouble. The spirit disappeared back into mist, which soon dissipated.

"Elissa, you might as well sit down and rest," Smeme said. "This could take some time."

Elissa sat. Smeme also made himself more comfortable. Teris remained on guard.

"How come you can summon Athena's spirit?" Elissa asked.

"As I told you: I know some things," Smeme smiled.

Teris looked over at Smeme with interest.

"Those 'things' certainly seem to have been helpful today!" Elissa observed wryly.

Smeme smiled again.

The team waited. With the Harpies standing nearby, no one was going anywhere anytime soon!

In Olympus, Athena went to see Themis in her beautiful palace. Themis was sitting in one of the rooms, awaiting the arrival of the evildoer for judgment. She welcomed Athena and offered her a chair.

"Thank you for seeing me, noble Themis," Athena began. "I have come to ask you what Elissa, daughter of Yorgos of Oe, from Attica, where my faithful city Athens lies, has done."

"I have heard that she has broken the natural order and that she plans to challenge the laws of the Gods to our faces," Themis replied. "I have sent my Harpies to fetch her for immediate judgment."

Athena considered. "As goddesses, we need to stick together," she said. "We need to support each other so that good will always be done."

Themis stared at Athena coldly, apparently unmoved by her statements.

Athena thought again. "Very well. Despite what you may have heard, and I don't know from whom,

Elissa has done nothing wrong. Elissa prayed to me and made suitable offerings several times and I blessed her journey."

Themis seemed interested.

Athena continued: "Elissa's journey is to find out the truth about how the world should be run. She wants to consult the Gods so that there would be no misunderstanding. It is a kind of law and order question, if you like."

Themis appeared to be considering the idea.

"I believe that you, correct me if I am wrong or am saying this the wrong way, would support any quest to determine and live by what is good and right?" Athena proposed.

Themis thought. She toyed with her scales of justice, moving the plates up and down.

"You have said it well, wise Athena," Themis finally answered. "It is a good case. We will be better able to determine the guilt or innocence of this kore after she has completed her quest and consulted with us Gods. If she chooses to lead a good and proper life after the consultation then we will know that no judgment is needed against her. Let her continue to honor you by being left free to complete the quest for which she asked your permission."

"I thank you," Athena bowed and departed.

Themis went into a meditative trance that enabled her to summon the Harpies back to Olympus. The Harpies heard Themis's command and took off from the clearing, shrieking with disappointment as they flew away. Teris watched them go, making sure that there would be no surprise return. Elissa and Smeme also stood and watched the Harpies disappear into the distance.

The mist formed again on the mountainside and flowed down toward the team. The spirit of Athena reappeared and turned to Elissa.

"You, Elissa of Attica, have my blessing to continue to try to complete your noble mission," the spirit said. "But be warned! There may be obstacles to overcome that may have originated from unexpected sources."

The tall spirit gave a solemn nod to Smeme and then dissipated back into the mist.

The three travelers walked onwards along the mountain track as it continued to descend. Soon they arrived at a vast plain. The track widened further and they were able to proceed more quickly. The track joined a country road. After some hours of walking, the travelers arrived at a roadside inn. The three took the opportunity for some well-deserved rest. They entered the inn and ordered some rooms and an evening meal.

After the meal, Elissa excused herself, saying that she was exhausted by all the recent events, and went to her room to sleep. Teris and Smeme decided to stay up for a little longer. They sat outside, as the evening was still quite warm, and ordered wine mixed with water.

"You know, I misjudged you, Smeme," Teris said.

"You did?" Smeme replied in an incredulous tone, but his eyes were twinkling.

"Yes. I thought you were a bit of a charlatan, to be honest. But it seems that Athena does not think so!" said Teris.

"I am not sure what old gray eyes thinks of me," said Smeme, "but she was kind enough to answer our prayer. Perhaps it was because Elissa is such a fine young lady?"

Teris nodded. "Perhaps so," he said.

The pair continued to sit and drink for some time. As they sat drinking, an attractive young woman came walking along the road. She saw the drinking pair in front of the inn and approached them.

"Hello stranger," the young woman said to Teris. "We don't often see handsome warriors like yourself in these parts! May I sit with you for a while, just to enjoy your company?"

Teris observed the woman's great beauty, which was enhanced by the wine he had been drinking.

"Sure. You are welcome, young lady," Teris invited, making room for her on the bench. As she sat down, an intoxicating cloud of musk and flowery scents enveloped Teris. He ordered another cup so the young woman could share the wine.

Smeme sat quietly, minding his own business.

The young woman accepted the wine and sat making eyes at Teris. Her beauty entranced Teris and he could not look away. What fine young ladies you could find out here in the countryside!

After some time the young woman smiled at Teris and said: "Maybe we could take a walk in the woods, just the two of us? You see, I have something personal that I would like to show you."

Teris's heart fluttered. Something personal? Could this be his lucky night? He stood up to go.

Smeme watched the scene calmly. But suddenly he wondered: what was going on? Is this what it seemed to be? Was this just some casual dalliance with a loose woman, or was it something more? Could this be one of those unexpected obstacles that the spirit of old gray eyes had warned about? He thought back over his experiences: what did his hard-won wisdom tell him? He knew!

Smeme grabbed hold of Teris's arm. Teris looked around.

"Come with me for a moment," Smeme said. "I want to tell you something."

Teris was confused. He looked at the waiting woman. She smiled demurely.

"I will just be a moment," Teris said. "I will join you soon."

The young woman nodded happily.

Smeme took Teris into the inn and over to a quiet corner of the room.

"That bewitching young lady reminds me of the story of Empusa," Smeme said.

"Empusa?" Teris inquired.

"Empusa has the ability to turn herself into a beautiful woman at night," Smeme explained. "She seduces men and takes them aside. Then, when they are alone, she attacks them and drinks their blood and eats their flesh."

"What!" Teris exclaimed. "Is that her out there?"

"I don't know for sure," Smeme replied. "But it is an amazing coincidence after what old gray eyes warned."

"How dare she try to do that to me!" Teris shouted. "I am going to get my spear and teach her a lesson she'll never forget!"

Teris got up to leave, but Smeme grabbed his arm again.

"You have high spirits, young warrior, but that won't work," Smeme said. "Empusa is far too powerful a monster to be overcome by human force."

"I don't care," Teris replied. "I am going to get her anyway."

Smeme stood and held both of Teris's arms.

"Leave this to me," Smeme instructed.

Smeme went outside and approached the beautiful young woman. Teris followed behind. The woman stood up, looking questioningly at Smeme.

"You, Empusa, are an ugly woman who has never told the truth in her life," Smeme accused. "You are famous far and wide for being a deceiver of no importance and without an iota of honor."

The young woman was enraged by these accusations. She tried to speak but suddenly metamorphosed into a hideously deformed creature that stood on a single donkey's leg. Teris could not believe what he was seeing. So this was the beautiful young woman with whom he was going to take a romantic stroll!

Empusa stared at the two men with big black eyes. She scowled at them, but her cover was blown. There was nothing to do but flee. She hopped away into the dark woods.

Smeme watched the creature go and then turned and resumed his seat at the outdoor table. He picked up his cup and took a swig of the diluted wine.

Teris remained where he was standing, feeling dumbfounded. After a while, he also resumed his seat next to Smeme. It must be safe, he reasoned, if Smeme thinks so.

"Smeme," Teris said, "you've done it again! You have amazed me."

"I'm glad you think so," Smeme replied. "I think I have amazed myself too! I thought my days were over."

"You did? But you were amazing, Smeme. I am so glad that you have come with us to help us," Teris enthused.

"You've done all right yourself, young man," Smeme replied. "I only hope we can survive the next challenge we will have to face."

"You think there will be more?" Teris blurted out. "But, of course, you are right," he said more calmly.

Smeme raised his eyebrows in reply.

"Why didn't Empusa attack us, Smeme? Why did she run away?" Teris asked.

"That was my gamble," Smeme replied. "Long ago, on my travels, I heard a story which claimed that the one thing Empusa could not stand was to be slandered. If she was slandered, she had no choice but to run away. I was gambling that the story had some truth to it!"

"Your gamble paid off!" Teris laughed, then suddenly became thoughtful. "You know, if it hadn't been for you, I might have gone off with that thing. A great help to Elissa that would have been!"

"Yes," Smeme agreed. "You would have been eaten by that beauty!"

"I am so ashamed, Smeme. Please don't tell Elissa what I did."

"Of course I won't, Teris," Smeme replied. "It would be better if we don't bother her with this little incident."

Teris nodded seriously.

"Thank you, Smeme. I like Elissa. I wouldn't want her to hear about my behavior."

"Don't say another word, young warrior," said Smeme. "My lips are sealed."

The two shook hands and agreed that it would probably be best if they returned to their rooms and got some sleep before the next day's journey.

As he lay on his bed, Teris made a commitment to himself that he would never again drink too much. Better to keep a sound head than act like a fool, he thought, before he fell asleep.

After breakfast, the three left the inn and went on their way. They crossed a vast plain that had the occasional farm. As they walked, Smeme talked about the types of dangers that can come to strangers in the wild: bears, lions, wild boars, wolves, and so on. He carefully avoided mentioning any supernatural beings, or monsters, such as Empusa! Elissa listened happily.

Teris followed, watching alertly in every direction. You never knew what was coming these days, he thought.

"But, Smeme, why should we worry about wild animals now? With Athena on our side, no harm can come to us," Elissa objected.

"That is true," Smeme replied, "but she did warn us to be on our guard."

Teris gulped quietly behind them.

"Yes. And as she did, I will certainly be on my guard!" Elissa declared. She looked about herself, but it was just a fine sunny day on the plain, with some local people tending their farm nearby.

Elissa started to sing as they walked. She felt in high spirits after her long, innocent sleep.

Teris kept walking behind, watching everywhere.

After some hours they reached the end of the plain. They started to climb and entered a forested area that did not have any paths. Teris moved to the front and, using his knowledge of navigation, guided the team in the right direction.

Evening was approaching. The team set up camp for the night.

The next morning, the three had breakfast and continued slowly uphill through the forest.

They had been walking for a few hours when they noticed some loud noises coming from the woods ahead. It sounded like trees were crashing to the ground. Teris spotted a cave and the team went inside, just in case there was any danger. They stood in the cool shadow of the cave's entrance and looked out. Three enormous giants came into view. They wore clothes made from animal skins and had thick hair and long beards. Their lower bodies and bare feet were covered in scales. The giants were using their titanic strength to pull trees out of the ground, complete with their roots, and throw them as far as they could manage. Eventually, the giants got tired of pulling up the trees and sat down together.

"What you do next?" one of the giants asked the others.

"Dunno," one replied.

The third just shrugged.

"Nuttin' to do," the first giant complained.

The second giant looked around him. "Nuttin' to eat, nuttin' to do," he confirmed.

"Mebbee we make bonfire?" the third giant suggested.

"Okay," the others agreed.

The giants got up and started to drag all the uprooted trees to a clear rocky area near the cave. The team crept back from the cave's entrance, moving as quietly as they could. The giants propped the trees against each other, forming a standing circle so that they would burn quickly. They then gathered twigs and smaller branches, arranging them in orderly layers under the trees.

"It's going to be a huge bonfire. We'd better get out of here," Teris whispered.

"But how can we?" Elissa asked softly. "Do giants eat people?"

"I don't want to find out," Smeme whispered in reply. "They don't look too friendly."

"We'd better wait here quietly, out of view," Elissa suggested. "Perhaps the giants will go away."

Teris and Smeme agreed. There was no other choice.

The giants did not go away. They finished their bonfire preparations and were feeling tired. They decided to take a nap. The giants lay down around the unlit bonfire and quickly fell asleep, snoring so loudly that the earth seemed to vibrate around them.

Elissa crept to the front of the cave and went to sneak outside, but one of the giants was lying right across the entrance. Teris silently gestured to her to come further back into the cave. The three explored the walls of the cave in the dim light inside, looking for an opening, but they could not find one. The cave was shallow, with only one way out – the way they had come in!

The three were out of options. Perhaps, if they hid here overnight, the giants would not see them and would eventually leave, allowing the team to escape. But what if the bright light from the bonfire shone far into the cave and illuminated them? There was nowhere inside to hide. Surely they would be caught and eaten! There was no way they could fight creatures that big.

Smeme reminded Elissa and Teris that he had the invisibility cloak given to him by the Sphinx, but it was only big enough for one person to wear. There was not enough room under the cloak for all of them to escape.

"Smeme, you should at least save yourself," Elissa said. "Put on the cloak and go. Teris and I can take care of ourselves."

Smeme smiled. "It would be better if you escaped," he replied, handing the cloak to Elissa.

"Then who will protect me in the future?" Elissa smiled in return, handing the cloak back to Smeme.

Smeme turned to Teris. "Maybe you could go and get help?" he proposed.

"Against giants!" Teris retorted.

"Yes. Good point," Smeme conceded.

The giants had stopped snoring and started to stir. They stretched and yawned.

"We make fire now?" one giant asked.

"Too bright," another replied. "Wait till dark."

"Okay," the first giant said.

"Maybe when they light the fire we will be able to get away," Teris whispered. "It will be dark."

"It may be our only chance," Smeme agreed.

Elissa silently nodded.

"If only I had a spell for giants," Smeme muttered to himself. He took off his backpack and started rummaging inside it. A bronze spoon dropped out of the pack and clattered across the rocky floor.

The giants spun around.

"What that?" one giant asked. It went over to the cave entrance and peered inside.

Smeme waved to Elissa and Teris to get behind him. He pulled his pack closer and held the invisibility cloak in front of himself.

The giant stared into the dim cave. The cave mouth was too small for it to enter, but it pushed its head inside as far as it could. It could not see anything except the walls of the shallow cave. It went back to the group.

"Must been echo," the giant said.

"Of what?" one said. "Of your stomach rumbling!" he laughed.

The three giants laughed together.

Smeme put down the cloak. He carefully picked up the spoon and cautiously returned it to his backpack. He closed the pack's flap and tied it firmly shut.

The three crept to the rear of the cave and sat as quietly as they could.

Outside, the giants were sitting around the unlit bonfire, waiting for the sun to set.

"Hey, listen to this one!" one giant invited. "What is dumb and tasty?"

"I dunno," the second said.

"A human!" the first shouted.

They all laughed.

"Okay, how about this?" the third giant began. "What tastes better than cooked goat?"

The others shook their heads.

"A cooked man!" the third cried.

More loud laughter.

"Where do you cook a camper?" the first asked.

Shaking heads.

"On a campfire!"

"What about a hoplite?" the third added. "In the firelite!"

"If a human makes you spit… put them on a spit!" the second roared.

Hearty, raucous laughter.

"That good one!" the third giant approved.

The sun had set. Darkness was beginning to descend.

"Let's light bonfire now!" the giants cried with delight.

They struck huge flinty rocks against each other, creating a shower of sparks which dropped onto the waiting tinder. Soon the kindling was alight. The flames crept up among the twigs and lapped at the waiting trees. The fire grew bigger and bigger.

The giants danced gleefully around the mighty, roaring flames. Sparks gushed up into the air. The intense light of the fire cast immense shadows of the giants across the surrounding grass and trees.

The giants began to sing as they danced.

"Oora! Oora! Oora!
Oora Ray! Oora Ray! Oora Ray!
Ray Oh! Ray Oh! Ray!
Ooblarah! Ooooblahrah! Blarah!
Yah! Yah! Yah!
Oooooo!"

They repeated these lines over and over, laughing between each set.

After a few hours, the bonfire began to burn out. The last remnants of the trees had been reduced to glowing coals and ashes. The giants were exhausted by their exuberant dancing and singing. They lay down beside the coals to sleep.

The team took their chance to escape. Smeme held his invisibility cloak ready in front of him, just in case the giants woke up. Elissa and Teris kept behind him as they all crept out of the cave and away from the scene. They entered the dark forest nearby and carefully navigated through the trees, putting as much distance between themselves and the giants as they could manage. When they felt that they were safe enough, they stopped and rested for the night.

The next day, the team broke camp and resumed their journey. Teris guided them out of the mountains and down onto a large, unpopulated plain. By evening they were still crossing the plain and had to make camp there.

On the following day the weather remained fine. The three travelers continued across the plain, arriving at the foothills of more mountains in the afternoon. Guided by Teris, they climbed among the firs and other trees. There was a little time for hunting hares for dinner before night fell. Elissa's skill with her hunting javelin proved more than adequate, once again. They made a small fire and roasted the hares.

Morning came. More climbing was needed. Teris found a narrow track that seemed to be going in the right direction. He led the team along it. The track followed the ridgeline of the mountains. It rose slightly before starting to descend again. From the top of the rise, Teris looked ahead and could see the track winding along the ridgeline into the distance. He could just make out something sitting far away on the track. He called Smeme forward.

"There's something there," Teris pointed. "Can you make out what it is?"

Smeme peered into the distance. "These old eyes are not up to the task," Smeme said. "Perhaps Elissa?"

Elissa came forward. She shielded her eyes with her hand and squinted. "It looks like a gigantic snake," Elissa said.

"How gigantic?" Smeme asked.

"I am not really sure," Elissa replied, still peering into the distance. "I guess it is bigger than the trees standing near it. It has a lot of teeth!"

"That's a dragon," Smeme said. "We can't fight that."

Teris scanned the scene ahead, searching for a way around. The slopes on either side of the track were steep and densely wooded: it would not be possible to clamber along them. Unless they gave up and turned back, it looked like there was no choice but to confront the dragon.

"It seems that we are going to have to fight it," Teris observed. "Unless someone has a better idea."

"Perhaps it will fly away," Elissa suggested optimistically.

"It's a wonderful thought," mused Smeme.

Teris frowned.

Elissa squinted at the dragon again. "You know, I think it's waiting there on purpose. Like the Sphinx," she gulped. "Hey! Could this be one of those obstacles sent from unexpected sources that Athena warned us about?"

"Possibly, yes," said Smeme.

"Then it looks like those sources are mighty powerful ones!" Elissa gasped.

"We are going to have to confront that dragon," Teris interrupted. "There is no other way. I will fight it off and you two can run past."

"How can you fight a dragon on your own, Teris?" Elissa asked with concern.

"What else can I do?" Teris replied. "You will be safe," he claimed.

"That is very brave of you, young warrior," Smeme said, "but perhaps it could also be called a little foolish?"

Teris gazed calmly at Smeme.

"I have a different plan," Smeme continued. "I could prepare a powerful sleeping potion for the dragon. I will need to gather a few herbs and some bark from the forest around here and cook it up. There is, however, one fatal flaw in my plan: I have no idea how to get the dragon to drink it!" he laughed.

Teris and Elissa looked thoughtful.

"I could try to spear it with the potion," Teris suggested.

"No, the dragon has to drink it," Smeme explained.

"Then I could throw the potion into its mouth," Teris proposed.

"You would never be able to get that close, young warrior," Smeme said. "You would be fried by its fiery breath!"

"What would you suggest, then?" Teris asked.

"I could throw my javelin down its throat!" Elissa cried.

"You could?" Smeme said, looking amazed.

"Yes, she could," Teris confirmed.

Elissa smiled at the endorsement.

"But how will you get the opportunity?" Smeme asked.

"Teris, you will have to distract the dragon with your spear and kopis," Elissa said.

"It's a pity I didn't bring my shield," Teris moaned.

"Yes. But you will be all right, brave Teris!" Elissa encouraged.

Teris gave a grim smile.

"Then, when the dragon opens its mouth, I will throw my javelin with the potion attached down its throat!" Elissa laughed.

"It's an audacious plan, Elissa," Smeme said. "You would only get one chance before someone got fried!" He thought for a moment. "I will help distract the dragon by throwing rocks at it while I am wearing my invisibility cloak. That way you may be able to get closer without being noticed."

"So, that's our plan," said Teris.

"Yes," said Smeme. "But I would like to amend some of the details, if I may. For example, about your shield: it would be better if you had one. Perhaps we can borrow one from somewhere?"

"In the forest!" Teris retorted.

"Perhaps. Perhaps. We will see," Smeme replied mysteriously. "I will go and collect the materials for my potion now," he continued, and walked off among the trees.

Elissa and Teris moved off the track and hid behind some bushes where they could keep an eye on the dragon without being seen. The dragon was carefully watching the track in front of itself, ready to pounce on any creature that came into view. From the distance its scaly skin looked metallic. Its huge, razor-sharp teeth were like rows of lethal daggers, just waiting for the opportunity to tear a warrior's flesh apart.

Teris shuddered involuntarily.

Some hours passed. Teris and Elissa nibbled on their supplies while they waited. In the afternoon, Smeme returned from the forest. He was carrying a bag containing various herbs, pieces of bark, and fungi. He also carried a shield. He came over to Teris.

"Try this on for size," Smeme invited.

Teris stared at the shield in disbelief. There was an owl painted on its metal face.

"Where did you get this?" Teris asked.

"Gray eyes lent it to me," Smeme replied. "We have to give it back after the battle."

"That's amazing!" Elissa marveled.

Teris stood and put his left arm into the shield's straps. The shield felt light yet strong. Fighting would be a lot easier with this master creation!

Teris picked up his spear and made some practice thrusts with it while turning his body and stepping back and forward, moving the shield into the most effective defensive position with each change in his posture. He smiled with satisfaction.

"Thank you, Smeme. I will make good use of this!" Teris said.

"I look forward to seeing that!" Smeme replied.

Smeme then got some wood and tinder together and made a modest fire. He took a small pot out of his backpack and dropped in cut herbs, crumbled fungi and crushed pieces of bark. He poured some water from a wineskin into the pot and started cooking the mixture over the fire. A pungent medicinal smell arose from the mixture as it boiled. Smeme kept stirring and simmering the concoction until it turned gelatinous and sticky. He set it aside to cool.

While Smeme was waiting for the mixture to cool down, he went and sat next to Elissa.

"This is a great quest you are on," Smeme said.

"Is it?" Elissa said. "Sometimes I am not so sure."

"No, you should be," Smeme said. "Only the most noble of individuals seeks to understand the will of the Gods and live by it."

Elissa smiled thinly.

"Smeme is right," Teris interjected. "It is a noble quest."

"But is it noble to endanger your friends?" Elissa asked.

"What danger?" Teris grinned. "With your javelin-throwing skills that dragon is as good as asleep right now!"

"Thank you. I hope so!" Elissa smiled.

"Perhaps you should prepare yourself?" Smeme suggested.

"Yes, you are right!" Elissa replied. She took her javelin and went back down the track to a flatter, more open area where she could warm up and practice her throwing out of sight of the dragon.

"She is a fine warrior maiden," Smeme said admiringly to Teris.

Teris nodded.

"How did you get this shield?" Teris asked.

"That is a good question, Teris, but I'm afraid the answer must remain between me and gray eyes," Smeme replied.

Teris nodded quietly, studying the owl painted on the face of the shield.

Smeme went and checked his potion. It was cool enough to use now. He walked down the track and called to Elissa to bring her javelin. Elissa came back from her practicing and handed her hunting javelin to Smeme. Smeme took the javelin and applied the sticky mixture to its tip with the help of his bronze spoon.

"That should be enough," Smeme said. "Be careful not to cut yourself on this. It would put you into a sleep from which you would never wake!" Smeme warned.

"I will," Elissa declared confidently.

Smeme kicked earth over the fire, returned his belongings to his backpack and put it on. He turned to Teris.

"Are you ready, young man?" Smeme asked Teris.

Teris nodded. Keeping his kopis sheathed by his side, Teris took up the shield, inserted his left arm through its straps, grasping it firmly, and picked up his spear.

Smeme wrapped himself in his invisibility cloak.

"Let's go!" Smeme's voice came from the air.

The three headed along the mountain track toward the dragon. When they got closer, Elissa crept among the trees on the edge of the track, doing her best to keep out of sight.

The dragon spotted Teris approaching fearlessly in the middle of the track. Elissa stayed out of view, her javelin ready in its throwing strap. The dragon sized up Teris.

"You cannot pass!" the dragon roared.

"Who says so?" Teris demanded loudly.

The dragon snorted. Some acrid tendrils of smoke escaped from its nostrils.

"That is not for you to know, little boy," the dragon replied.

"Move aside, dragon without a name!" Teris commanded. "Or be prepared to fight!"

The dragon leaped forward, fire streaming from its gaping mouth. Teris lifted his borrowed shield and held it in front of him. The flames flowed harmlessly around its protective surface. Teris pointed his spear at the dragon's chest and took a step forward. The dragon went to strike him with its huge head, but a rock flew through the air and hit it in the eye. The dragon spun its head around but could not see where the rock had come from.

Another rock appeared from the air and struck the dragon on the nose.

"What?" the dragon roared angrily.

Teris lunged forward, thrusting his spear into the dragon's chest, but the iron tip just bounced off the scaly skin.

Another blast of flame engulfed Teris, deflected by his extraordinary shield.

The dragon's head knocked against the shield and Teris fell onto his back.

The dragon moved in for the kill. It opened its mouth wide and gave out a roar of triumph... a javelin suddenly shot down its throat.

Elissa stood victorious, admiring her throw. She had done it! She had hit the mark!

The dragon was stunned by this new development. It gulped and looked all around itself. Where had that little toothpick come from? It felt groggy and wobbled back and forth. Its head slumped to the ground. The slitted eyes went blank. It was fast asleep.

Teris got back onto his feet. Smeme appeared from the air beside Teris as he removed his cloak. Elissa ran up to them.

"One javelin down!" she laughed.

Smeme signaled to her to keep quiet. They crept past the sleeping dragon and quickly put some distance between it and themselves before the sun set.

The next day the team awoke many stadia down the mountain track. Teris looked for his shield but it was gone. Smeme advised him that it had been returned to its lender. The three had breakfast and soon were on their way.

The forests got thinner and thinner, giving way to more open areas, which were hilly and rocky. There was no chance of taking cover here if something should choose to attack them.

Elissa felt lost without her hunting javelin. How could she fight off dragons now? And there was nothing effective for her to hunt with. How would they eat?

Smeme suggested that they buy a new javelin at the next settlement they came to. This should solve the problem.

Teris was missing that amazing fireproof shield. He wondered privately if he would ever see the like of it again.

The team kept walking. It was still a long way to Mount Olympus. There was no time to waste!

4. AEOLUS

In Olympus, Zeus had heard rumors about Elissa and her journey. The mighty leader of all the Gods had been told that this young, inexperienced, mortal kore had the audacity to imagine that she had rights over the Gods. She, a mere woman, wanted to challenge the laws of society and question the Gods to their faces, accusing them of hubris against humankind. What cheek! What gall! What impudence! Such behavior could not continue unopposed. He sent for Aeolus, to speak to him in secret.

Aeolus came in answer to Zeus's summons. He bowed before the great king.

"What is your wish, oh Supreme Leader of the Gods?" Aeolus asked.

"My wish is that you seek out Elissa, daughter of Yorgos of Oe of Attica, and when you find her and her party, you blow your strongest and bitterest wind on them and drive them back from whence they came!" Zeus decreed.

"I will return to my island of Aeolia and get my bag of wind at once, Great One!" Aeolus declared, bowing low and departing swiftly.

Aeolus flew back to his enchanted island, collected his huge shepherd's bag of winds, and went in search of the reprobates. Flying fast on the wind, Aeolus soon found Elissa and her party of trouble-makers. They were crossing a barren rocky area between the mountain peaks. Aeolus opened his bag and instructed Boreas, the north wind, to come out and blow as fiercely as he could on Elissa and her party, forcing them to turn back.

Boreas leaped out of the bag, flapping his wings as he hovered in the air. His long white beard dangled down toward the ground, his cloak billowed around him. He took out a large conch shell and started to blow through it. A strong, cold wind burst forth. It swept across the rocky ground, howling as it blew straight into the faces of Elissa and her friends. They shivered in its icy blast.

Elissa and Smeme were knocked to the ground by the powerful wind. They crawled on all fours, searching for some shelter on the rocky hilltop. Teris leaned into the wind but could only inch forward slowly. The three found a shallow depression in the surface of the rocks and crept into it. The wind blew above them. They settled down and waited for it to pass.

Night came and the wind was still blowing. The team rummaged inside their packs and put together a cold meal. They ate lying down while the freezing wind roared above them. After the meal they made themselves as comfortable as they could on the stony ground. Using their packs as pillows, they tried to get some sleep.

Day came and the freezing gale was still blasting above them at full force.

"This must be a windy part of the country!" Smeme shouted. "But it can't go on forever. You remember that when we started across this area there was no wind?"

"That's right!" Teris yelled, then frowned. "But what do I know about the weather up north?"

"Let's wait it out!" Smeme suggested.

"Yes, let's!" Elissa and Teris agreed loudly.

The day passed. The wind continued to howl above and around them. The team endured as best as they could. There was no choice: they weren't going anywhere.

Another night and still the wind blew. Their supplies had run out now, but it was impossible to leave the depression in the rocks and go hunting. The three got what meager sleep they could.

The sun rose and another day began. The three were hungry, cold and exhausted. Going without food and being unable to sleep properly on the stony ground had taken its toll. If only they could have lit a fire to drive out the cold!

"This is really strange," Elissa observed. "Could this be another of those unexpected obstacles that come from who knows where?"

"Yes, where does it come from?" Smeme replied. "Good point!"

"It is not natural, this wind," said Teris thoughtfully. "It cannot be. How could it last so long?"

"In that case, let's pray," suggested Smeme.

The three prayed as best as they could, without offerings and forced to keep lying flat in the depression. They prayed to all the Gods for help. They prayed sincerely and hard. This was their last hope.

In Olympus, the desperate prayers of the three reached Hera, the wife of Zeus and Queen of Heaven. She wondered at what she was hearing. Who were these mortals and what was happening with the wind? Was some God intervening and why? She heard one of the mortals, a young kore, mention Athena many times in her prayers. Hera sent for Athena to see if the goddess could explain.

Athena came to Hera's throne room and bowed to her queen.

"What is this that I am hearing from this young kore and her companions?" Hera asked. "What is the quest she keeps mentioning along with your name? Do you know why the wind may be stopping them?"

Athena listened to the ongoing prayers.

"This is Elissa, a faithful follower of mine," Athena replied. "This mortal is on a quest to find out the true way for a human woman to live according to the will of the Gods. She has prayed to me often about this and I have endorsed her quest."

"That sounds eminently respectable," Hera said. "But what is this wind that is stopping her?"

"I do not know, My Queen," Athena replied.

"Bring me Aeolus," Hera instructed her attending servants.

Hera's celestial servants promptly fetched Aeolus from his enchanted island. Aeolus stood before Hera, with his bag of winds clasped by his side.

"How can I be of service to you, Great Queen of Heaven?" Aeolus said, bowing low.

"What is going on with the wind?" Hera asked.

"Nothing that I can reveal, Queen of Olympus," Aeolus replied, bowing even lower.

"Then kindly return the winds to normal," Hera directed.

"Yes, Great Goddess. At once!" Aeolus answered and rapidly departed.

Aeolus flew to the mountains where Boreas was still blowing fiercely through his conch shell at Elissa and her party.

"Stop!" Aeolus commanded. "Get back into the bag."

Aeolus opened his huge bag of winds and Boreas leaped inside. Aeolus flew away, back to his enchanted island, Aeolia.

Elissa, Teris and Smeme noticed that the howling cold gale had eased back to a normal pleasant breeze.

"Athena be praised!" Elissa cried. "The wind is gone!"

"All hail Athena and the Gods!" Smeme called to the heavens.

Teris nodded. Under his breath, so that the others couldn't hear, he thanked the Gods for helping his noble friend, Elissa.

The three stood up. They stretched their stiff backs and rubbed their aching limbs.

"It's good to be able to stand again," Elissa said.

"Indeed. If a little painful!" Smeme joked.

When they felt that they had recovered sufficiently, they picked up their belongings, put on their packs, and resumed their journey.

In Olympus, Zeus was raging. He roared for Aeolus to come immediately into his presence. At once! Aeolus flew as quickly as he could back to Olympus. He rushed into Zeus's throne room and flung himself on the floor.

"What have you done! You miserable worm!" Zeus thundered. He stormed up and down in front of Aeolus's prostrate body.

"Great King of the Gods," Aeolus answered, "I had to stop the wind as it was Hera herself who asked me."

"My wife!" Zeus exclaimed. "Why should she ask you?"

"I do not know, Great Ruler of Heaven," Aeolus replied.

"Hmmm, never mind," Zeus said, suddenly calm. "You may leave me." He waved for Aeolus to go.

Aeolus took his chance to escape the great God's terrifying wrath and scuttled hurriedly away.

Zeus returned to his throne and sat with his head in his hands, brooding deeply.

Elissa, Teris and Smeme were feeling satisfied. They had full stomachs, thanks to a successful hunt, and had covered many stadia through the mountains. After the wind abated, nothing else had stood in their way. Mount Olympus looked closer than ever.

They had come across a village on the route and had taken the opportunity to buy a new hunting javelin for Elissa. She felt a lot better having a useful weapon in her hand again. You never knew when it would be needed. Teris had declined the purchase of a shield. He was already carrying a lot in his backpack, and his kopis and double-ended spear were heavy. In any case, a normal shield was also quite weighty, not like the extraordinary one that Smeme had borrowed for him. A wealthy warrior would have had his shield carried to the battle by a slave or retainer. He wouldn't carry it all that way by himself. He needed to conserve his strength for fighting. But now there was no one in the party that Teris would ask to be his porter!

Elissa walked confidently ahead. She could not wait to reach her goal. Teris and Smeme felt less certain, but they kept their doubts to themselves. They did not want to bring Elissa down.

In Olympus, Zeus had been sitting and thinking and was getting angrier and angrier. This group of impious troublemakers was getting on his nerves. They had no right to go on this quest without his consent. Olympus was his place, not theirs! Strange mortals could not turn up and treat this like some kind of holiday destination, created just for their pleasure. This was his home and the abode of the Gods, not some pathetic human city! You had to be invited… and why would any God invite creatures like these mortals here? Which reminded him that it was his own wife who had supported them against him. Only, she hadn't known it was on his orders that the party was stopped. He granted her that. Well, something had to be done. But it had better be done in a way that Hera would not find out about. There was no sense in adding to the existing trouble at home!

Zeus had an idea. He summoned Phobos, the personification of fear, to meet him in his private room.

The young male god with mane-like hair, eyes of flame, and a row of bared teeth, entered his grandfather's private room.

"What can I do for you, King of All the Gods?" Phobos asked.

Zeus suppressed a slight shudder at the sight of his terrifying grandson. He was not one to feel panic and fear!

"Greetings, Phobos," Zeus replied. "You are very welcome here. I want you to do a small favor for me, but to do it in secret, to be known only to you and me."

Phobos kindly nodded his assent, yet the gesture seemed strangely menacing.

"Thank you for your support. I want you to go and find a certain group of three travelers."

"Yes?" said Phobos.

"Yes. Go and find them, this Elissa and her friends, and strike fear into them such as they have never known before," said Zeus.

"I can do that," Phobos grinned, his long rows of white teeth flashing.

Zeus shuddered.

"That's wonderful," Zeus said. "Strike fear into them so that they panic and turn back from their sacrilegious journey to our holy domain. I want them to flee. I want them to run away, back to the filthy human realm that they dared to venture forth from. Back to their mortal homes, where they can live their futile little lives and die and go down into Tartarus for their deserved punishment, for all I care. Could you do that for me?"

"I would be honored, Great Father Zeus," Phobos bowed politely, yet sinisterly.

Phobos left Zeus's private room, crossed through the throne room, and exited Zeus's palace in search of the travelers.

Zeus stood with his hands on his hips, feeling a lot better than he had in days. Things were going well. This was going to be good!

Outside the palace, Phobos paused for a moment to think. How could he find these elusive travelers of Zeus? Where could they be? There was only one thing to do. If you wanted to know something about travelers, you should ask Hermes, the God who supported them. He set off to find Hermes.

Hermes was walking through the gold-paved streets of Olympus when Phobos caught up with him.

"Hermes!" Phobos called threateningly.

Hermes looked around. He saw Phobos approaching him and gave an involuntary shudder. That God was so creepy!

"Yes, Phobos?" Hermes said.

"It is good to see you," Phobos replied, sounding like he was making some sort of dark private joke. "Would you be able to help me? I am looking for some mortals. I can't tell you why. It would have to remain our secret."

"Okay," said Hermes hesitatingly. "Who are you looking for?"

Phobos glanced up and down the street, his flaming eyes making sure that no one was in earshot.

"I need to find Elissa and her party of two. Does that ring any bells?" Phobos said.

"Yes, I know them. Elissa, daughter of Yorgos of Oe in Attica, and Teris and Smeme," Hermes replied.

"Could you tell me where they are?" Phobos smiled, with his flashing white teeth.

"Yes, of course," Hermes said.

Hermes gave directions to Phobos. Phobos thanked him, reminded Hermes that this was just between the two of them, and then set off on his mission.

Hermes shook his head. He never liked meeting that God. He continued walking along the golden street. As he turned a corner, he saw his half-brother, Apollo.

"Apollo! Well met!" Hermes called.

"Greetings, Hermes!" Apollo replied.

The two gave each other a manly embrace.

"I just met Phobos," Hermes said.

"Oh yes?" said Apollo.

"He swore me to secrecy, but I am disturbed," Hermes continued.

"He does that to everyone," Apollo observed.

"Yes, he does, doesn't he! Anyway, that is not what disturbed me. He said he had to find some mortals but I was not to know why."

"Which mortals?" Apollo asked.

"You won't spread it around that I told you?" Hermes checked.

"No, you can trust me," Apollo confirmed.

Hermes nodded.

"Elissa, daughter of Yorgos of Oe in Attica. Also, her companions: Teris, son of Herodotos of Oe, and Smeme, magos and follower of Athena," Hermes answered.

"I know her," Apollo said. "Teris presented her question to me at Delphi."

"He did?"

"Yes. How interesting," Apollo said thoughtfully. "Anyway, it is nothing to do with us," he continued more brightly. "Thanks for sharing your secret with me. I must get on now. I'll talk to you later."

Apollo waved and went on his way.

The next morning, the team had a hearty breakfast and resumed their journey. Elissa sang as she walked ahead with Smeme. She was feeling fine. Teris followed behind, looking around warily.

"I think we are going to have smooth sailing now," Elissa said. "What could be worse than a dragon?" she asked.

"I am not sure," Smeme said.

"Come on!" Elissa replied. "We defeated it together, so we can defeat anything that comes our way!" she claimed.

"Anything they throw at us?" said Smeme. "I am not so sure."

"You will be," said Elissa, "when you see us beating it!"

"Okay," said Smeme. "I look forward to seeing that."

Teris frowned quietly behind them, still looking everywhere.

"You see," Elissa continued, "if it was a dragon we would put it to sleep. If it was like a set of giants we would sneak away behind your invisibility cloak. If it was a bunch of thugs, Teris would chase them away with his heroic warrior skills. If it was a riddle, you would answer it easily!"

"I would?" said Smeme. "Perhaps I would."

"And if it was a mistake from the heavens we would pray to Athena and she would help us," Elissa proposed.

"She might," Teris muttered gruffly behind them.

Phobos was flying invisibly in the direction that Hermes had given him. He spotted the party and descended toward them. He could hear Elissa's happy, confident tone. "We'll soon see about that!" he said to himself.

Phobos hovered invisibly above the group. He exerted his godly power over them.

Elissa and Teris suddenly felt afraid. Elissa stopped her chatter and looked around herself in terror. The day was sunny, with only a handful of white fluffy clouds floating high and free in the bright blue sky, yet Elissa felt that she was in the depths of night, in the dark of a starless midnight, with unseen dangers lurking all around her. Teris felt an irrational desire to run – but to run where? And from what? He could not determine where the threat was coming from. In any case, warriors did not run!

Even Smeme was feeling afraid. Why? Why did he feel like this? This must be a dark power that was about to confront them. Perhaps this would be the last moments of their lives.

The three probed the sky and looked all around, searching for the danger. Unconsciously, they formed a circle with their backs pressed together, their weapons facing outward and Smeme's spells at the ready.

"I wish I had bought that shield now!" Teris lamented. He scanned the surroundings frantically for the imminent attack.

"I don't know what spell to use to protect us," Smeme moaned. "I don't know what is coming!" His eyes combed the tranquil scenery, expecting at any moment to see the overpowering enemy rushing forward to destroy them.

Elissa peered into the forest and sky. Where was the target for her new javelin? Where would the menace come from? What if it was too powerful for her? What if she just froze and couldn't do anything when it appeared?

Elissa felt the terror of what might happen grow until it started to overwhelm her. What if the beast is huge, with multiple savage heads? What if all the party freezes and no one can do anything? This is ridiculous! she suddenly thought. There is nothing there. I can't see anything.

No, it is a sunny, clear day, out in nature, with nothing going wrong at all. Nothing out of the ordinary is happening here. In a scene like this, the only thing we need to fear is fear itself!

And is fear a thing that a person needs to fear? It is only the fear of fear that we need to worry about! This thought made her laugh.

Smeme and Teris looked around. What was wrong with Elissa? She was laughing out loud.

"Don't you see," Elissa said, breaking the circle and turning to face them. "There is nothing there. It's all in our minds. The only thing that we need to fear here is fear itself!"

Smeme nodded. "You are right, Elissa," he said. "This must be some kind of spell that we are under."

Teris threw his spear to the ground.

"Okay," Teris shouted, "fight me to my face, hand-to-hand combat, trickster! If you dare!"

Hovering above them, Phobos saw that his spell was broken. He flew down to the ground in front of the team and made himself visible. He stood huge and tall before them, with his flaming eyes and flashing white teeth, his hair resembling the mane of a lion.

"You have seen through my little trick today!" Phobos thundered. "But don't think that you will be so lucky in the future! I admire your fearlessness, there are very few who could match you, but I, Phobos, am the god of fear, so don't think that you will always escape me! Yet... I do admire Elissa's strength of character... unexpected in a mortal woman," he conceded.

"Consider yourselves lucky that my brother, Deimos, was not here with me today!" Phobos continued. "I depart and leave you in peace for now. Farewell, brave warriors!" he called, as he ascended into the sky.

The team watched as Phobos flew away, quickly disappearing from view.

"That was amazing, Elissa!" said Teris.

"Thank you, Teris. It was nothing really," Elissa replied. "As soon as I realized that we were feeling afraid for no reason, I could see a way out."

"You were most impressive, young kore," said Smeme. "I think you have a noble future."

"Thank you, Smeme. I don't know what I will have in the future, but it will be all the better for having met the two of you!" Elissa replied.

The three smiled and bowed to each other. Teris picked up his spear and the party resumed their journey. Evening came and they made camp for the night. They prepared and ate their dinner and immediately afterward lay down to rest. Soon they were all fast asleep.

During the night, a bright light and whooshing noise woke all the party. Flying through the air toward them was a glowing figure wearing a winged helmet and winged golden sandals. The wings flapped rapidly, enabling the young male God to move swiftly across the sky. He descended to the ground and stood before the party. He shone brightly, making the area around him look like it was in daylight. He pointed his ornate staff, with its two entwined serpents surmounted by wings, at Elissa.

"You are Elissa, daughter of Yorgos of Oe, who has taken this unprecedented quest to go to Mount Olympus to question the Gods?" the young God asked.

"I am," Elissa replied, stepping forward and bowing.

"I have been sent to give you this message from Apollo," the God said. "'The beast of the anti-truth will throw an unclimbable object in her path.'"

"Thank you, Hermes, for relaying this message to me," Elissa said, bowing again.

Hermes looked away coldly and departed. Darkness returned.

"'The beast of the anti-truth will throw an unclimbable object in your path?'" Smeme muttered. "Another riddle!" I wonder what that beast is, he thought to himself.

"Are you all right, Elissa?" Teris asked, stepping forward and facing his friend with a concerned expression.

"Yes, fine," Elissa replied casually. "It is puzzling... the message is puzzling. I wonder why it was passed to me? When we were in Delphi, the Oracle told us nothing, Teris."

"Well, Apollo has spoken directly now!" Smeme said. "Not through the Pythia. He must have really wanted you to get that message."

"Yeesss..." Elissa said slowly.

"Let's not worry about it now. Let's get some rest. We can think about it in the morning," Smeme suggested.

Elissa and Teris agreed and they all lay down to sleep.

As Elissa tried to return to sleep, she started wondering about the message. She couldn't get it out of her head. What was that beast that they would not be able to overcome because of its unclimbable object? What could the object be? She fell asleep still musing about that.

In the morning, the three had breakfast and resumed the topic of Apollo's mysterious message.

"Maybe my mission is doomed," Elissa began. "If there is to be an unclimbable object put in the way then what could we do about it? It would be unclimbable, so there is no way that we could reach our objective! The Gods would not lie, so Apollo must have predicted the truth with his oracle."

Smeme sat silently for a while, considering Elissa's argument.

"You must be right," Smeme finally said. "Apollo would not lie. So, Hermes' message must mean that there is no way that we could succeed. I cannot see any alternative to that conclusion. It is most confounding!"

Teris joined in.

"Elissa," Teris said, "the prophecy may be true, but I think that the exact future can never be known until it is right in front of you and you can touch it. I say: Why worry about something that you cannot see? Wait until we encounter this evil beast and we will see what we see then!"

"The young man may have something there, Elissa," Smeme conceded. "Maybe there is nothing for us to worry about until it happens! What good can we do by stewing over it?"

Elissa gave a thin smile to Teris and Smeme.

"I think you are right, Teris," Elissa said softly. "This may be the obstacle that we finally cannot overcome together, but at least we could go on and see what it is. Even if our quest ends there, it would be pointless to turn back now."

Teris and Smeme expressed their agreement. The three packed their belongings and continued on their journey.

After some hours of walking, the team came across an old abandoned altar to Hera near the path. Smeme asked if they could stop for a while so he could make some offerings there. Teris and Elissa agreed. Smeme collected some wildflowers and also took a small amphora of honey from his pack. He poured the honey onto the altar and placed the wildflowers around it. He then raised his hands toward the sky in prayer.

Smeme asked Hera and the other Gods to please support Elissa in her quest to find their holy truth, and to help her overcome the beast of the anti-truth, with its unclimbable object, as per the wise prophecy that they had received from the great and good Apollo. If it be their will, for it is the duty of man to live by and obey the will of the Gods.

Smeme's fervent prayer floated up into the heavens and was, in time, heard there by Hera, Apollo, Artemis, Athena and Hermes.

Artemis, the Goddess who protected women, wondered what the prayer was about. Who was this woman who needed help in finding the holy truth of the Gods? She hurried to the palace of her twin brother, Apollo, and asked him what his prophecy was based on.

"I don't know anything about it!" Apollo answered. "I never made such a prophecy. The last thing I relayed to Elissa, daughter of Yorgos of Attica, was that I did not have any meaningful message for her that day. I have never said anything since."

Artemis became agitated.

"What is happening then, dear brother! Who is this Elissa? What is happening with her?" she demanded.

"I only know that she sent her representative to ask me a question at Delphi," Apollo explained. "She wanted to know if she should continue on her quest to go to Mount Olympus to consult the Gods," he added.

"And you said that you didn't have any meaningful message for her that day?" Artemis asked.

"Yes, basically," Apollo replied. "I thought that the decision should be up to her, not us, so I let her decide by sending her no meaningful message."

"Loxias!" Artemis accused.

"Of course, dear sister," Apollo smiled. "That is my famous nature!"

Apollo thought for a moment.

"Hermes keeps track of travelers," Apollo said. "I will go and ask him if he knows what Elissa chose to do. Wait here; I shouldn't be long."

Apollo left Artemis and went in search of Hermes. He found Hermes on the street near Zeus's palace.

"Hail, Hermes!" Apollo called.

"Hail, Apollo!" Hermes called back.

"Hermes, I would like to ask you a question," Apollo said.

Hermes nodded.

"You have heard of the traveler, Elissa, daughter of Yorgos of Attica. We spoke about her earlier," Apollo said.

Hermes considered. "Yes, I remember," he replied after a while. "I know all travelers."

"Good! Do you know where she is now?"

"Yes, I am keeping track of her," Hermes said. "And watching over her," he added.

"Great!" Apollo said. "My sister was worried, but if you are watching over her then all is okay. Thank you for your help."

Apollo left Hermes and returned to his palace, where Artemis was waiting.

"There's nothing to worry about, sister," Apollo told Artemis. "Elissa is traveling and Hermes is watching over her."

"Is Hermes protecting Elissa, dear brother?" Artemis asked.

"He is the protector of all faithful travelers, dear sister," Apollo replied. "She is in good hands."

"Yes, you are right," Artemis agreed. "That is obvious and must be so."

Artemis returned to her palace. She sat on a golden chair to rest, but worrying thoughts came to her mind. Why did the magos, Smeme, think that the prophecy had been sent by her brother Apollo? Who or what had given the prophecy to him? There must be some deceptive spirit at work here.

Hermes was feeling agitated after his discussion with Apollo. He could not set his mind at rest. He had heard the talk around Olympus about Elissa and the prophecy, especially after Smeme's prayer to Hera and the Gods. He had not realized before that Elissa was a faithful follower of Athena, and had Athena's blessing for her quest. But now that he had heard Athena herself discussing the matter with some of the other Gods, how could he live with what he had done?

Hermes walked slowly to a corner near Hera's palace and watched carefully to ensure that no one was looking. When he saw that it was safe to enter, he took off his winged helmet and replaced it with his cap of invisibility. Unable to be seen, he cautiously snuck inside.

Hermes sought out Hera and waited until no attendant was nearby. He whispered into Hera's ear, asking if he could meet her in private. Hera nodded and sent everyone out of the room.

Hermes took off his cap of invisibility, his form immediately coming into view. He bowed deeply to Hera.

"Great Queen of Heaven, I thank you for seeing me in private," Hermes said. "May I beg of you that you do me the great honor of not discussing this meeting with anyone?"

Hera considered. "Very well," she said. "What is it that you want to tell me so secretly, Hermes?"

"Thank you, My Queen. "I have to tell you that it was your husband, Zeus, the leader of all the Gods, who commanded me to give the message to the mortal kore, Elissa, daughter of Yorgos of Attica," Hermes announced. "He, great leader and wise father that he is, compelled me to tell Elissa that the message came from Apollo, as she had previously gone to the Oracle at Delphi but had not received any prophecy there."

"Zeus? My husband? Why did he do that?" Hera demanded.

"I do not know, Queen of Olympus," Hermes replied. "I only know that he is very angry with Elissa and had sent Phobos to frighten her and her companions away."

Hera sat motionless, quietly contemplating.

"You may go, Hermes," Hera finally said. "I will tell no one of our conversation, as I agreed."

Hermes bowed, put on his invisibility cap, and silently departed.

❧❧❧❦❦❦

Smeme rejoined Elissa and Teris, who were waiting for the experienced magos a little distance away from the altar.

"I have prayed to the Gods for their support on your mission, Elissa," Smeme said. "I am certain that they heard my prayer. Everything should be okay for continuing your quest now."

"Thank you, Smeme. I am sure you are right," Elissa replied.

Hearing about Smeme's prayer set Elissa's dark thoughts in motion again. Smeme had prayed to the Gods to do something about the beast of the prophecy, but who was to say that they would be able to overcome it either? Where did such a beast of the anti-truth come from anyway, if it was not already known to the Gods? Wasn't everything known to the Gods: everything in existence? Then, if the Gods knew that there was a beast of the anti-truth that had the power to put unclimbable objects in people's paths, what could they do about it? In a way, the Gods had acknowledged that such a beast existed, and so they could not go against it because that would be going against what they knew of existence itself. This crazy, convoluted thought triggered a new idea in Elissa's mind: what if it was the Gods themselves who were sending the beast of the anti-truth?

If that was true then Apollo's message was not just a simple prophecy about the future: it was a statement of the Gods' intent. Apollo was telling Elissa that the Gods were against her, that they were opposing her. How could she overcome their great power? It was one thing to fight off a dragon or to answer a Sphinx's riddle, but quite another to try to go against the will of the Gods. Wouldn't resisting them be sacrilegious? Her quest was doomed. If she continued with her journey then she and her friends would surely be punished for their intransigence!

Elissa shared her concerns with Smeme and Teris.

Smeme considered Elissa's idea.

"I have seen many things over my life," Smeme said. "I have found that the power of the Gods is great beyond question, but the intention of their wills is not always easy to divine. You may think they are saying one thing yet find that they were saying another. Their thoughts can be like a mystery contained within another mystery. That is why I believe we should go to Mount Olympus to seek the truth that is the answer to your questions, Elissa. We cannot be sure whether the prophecy was about the will of the Gods or not until we go there," he advised.

"But what if it really is the will of the Gods?" Elissa objected. "Then we would be committing sacrilege. Do you want to take that risk?"

"You are making a good point, Elissa. I agree," Smeme replied. "But the Oracle did not say that the prophecy was about the will of the Gods. He said that the beast of the anti-truth would send the obstacle. Such a beast does not sound like one of the Gods to me."

"What do you think, Teris?" Elissa asked. "You haven't been saying much."

Teris considered slowly.

"I want what is best for you, Elissa," Teris finally replied. "That is all that I can say."

Elissa thought about her friends' statements carefully. She did not want to form an answer too hastily.

After a while, she spoke: "I thank you, Teris, for your concern for me. And I thank you, Smeme, for your wise and considered counsel. Let's continue walking and I will think about this some more, as we go," she proposed.

Smeme expressed his agreement. Teris simply nodded his assent.

The three went on. Teris remained watchful and alert as they proceeded, Elissa quietly thinking as she walked.

Elissa wondered what this beast of the anti-truth would be. She had not heard of such a thing in her short life, and, obviously, Smeme had no knowledge of it either. He would have told them if he knew what it was.

How could she know what the prophecy really meant? Was it saying that she would be going against the Gods in wanting to talk to them? Or was it not saying that? Why would the god Apollo, who would know about such things, have sent such a message to her… and in that manner?

This thinking was all very well, but it would never resolve the matter! If she remained obstinate and continued on her quest in spite of the warnings she had received then she may have stayed true to herself, but she would have endangered those who followed her unquestioningly.

Maybe it was time to grow up and give up. She should act her age: what would a responsible adult do?

Yet, giving up may be just what the beast of the anti-truth wanted. It was *anti-the-truth* after all! How could she resolve this issue? How could she find a solution to this mystery?

Elissa realized that the only sensible thing to do would be to consult an expert on oracles, which meant that she should return to the Temple of Apollo at Delphi and ask the priests there. The team would have to retrace their steps, maybe having to pass by that dragon again, but what choice was there? Going back was the only way that they could discover the truth.

Elissa stopped her friends and explained her thinking to them.

Smeme did not agree.

"We should continue forward and complete your quest," Smeme said. "Going backwards will achieve nothing."

Teris was not so sure.

"I don't know what is the best thing to do, Elissa," Teris said. "I will follow you wherever you choose to go."

Elissa hesitated. She did not want to endanger Teris or Smeme, but going back would have its dangers too! Who knew what might happen with the dragon the next time they encountered it? It would not be so easily fooled again. Teris may not be loaned the magical shield a second time. How would they defend themselves? Apart from the dragon, who knew what other monsters might be lurking behind them? She decided that the only thing to do for now was to keep walking forward and think some more.

Teris and Smeme silently followed Elissa.

Smeme was thinking about his own goals. He had been excited by the idea of going to Mount Olympus since he first overheard it. What an amazing adventure to be involved in! He could not wait to see what happened when Elissa spoke directly to the Gods of Olympus. What would they say? Would they respond angrily or would it be with the respect due to a genuinely sincere person?

Smeme moved closer to Teris and addressed him softly.

"What are your thoughts on this, Teris?" Smeme asked.

"I want to help and protect Elissa on her journey," Teris replied in a low voice.

"In which direction do you think her journey should be: forward or backward?" Smeme asked.

"I couldn't say," Teris replied. "I don't know anything about the Gods or quests. I only know that I want to protect Elissa to the best of my ability."

"That is commendable, young warrior," Smeme said. "But, may I ask: what is protection? What is protection if not to help Elissa reach her goal?"

"Yes, but in one piece. Alive," Teris retorted.

"You are right," Smeme said. "I stand corrected."

"Look," said Teris, "I have faith in Elissa. I think she is wiser than me and will make the right decision. When she finally does decide, I am ready to support her, come what may."

"You are inspiring, young warrior," Smeme replied. "In spite of all my years, I am learning a lot from you about trust and faith! I will adopt your example and follow Elissa wherever she finally chooses to go."

The three continued to walk toward Mount Olympus.

After a couple of hours they took a break for lunch.

"I have made a decision," Elissa said. "I think that the best thing for me to do would be to stop at the next temple I come to and consult the Gods there. That way I will have continued forward, hopefully not increasing my danger, and can still turn back if the Gods' answer wills it. Yet, if the Gods say I should keep going then at least I will have already traveled some of the way!

"Teris and Smeme, my dear friends, there is no need for you to come any further with me. There is a chance that the unclimbable obstacle will turn up before I reach the next temple, in which case we would all be doomed. I do not want you to take that risk for me. I want you both to keep safe. This is a risk I will face alone."

Smeme and Teris shook their heads.

"I disagree," Smeme said. "I have been thinking about the wise words that Teris shared with us before, regarding the future. It made me realize that the many things I have seen in my long life have taught me that what is to happen in the future can never be known with certainty by us mortals, until it finally happens! I will come with you and try, at the very least, to carry out our mission, whatever the Fates and the Gods have decided."

Elissa turned to Teris.

"I am not going to give up on you, Elissa," Teris said simply.

Elissa nodded to her friends.

"Well! I have done my absolute best to dissuade you both," Elissa said. "But I have to admit that I would be honored and happy to have your company. You are both such wonderful people!"

The three stood and proceeded on their way, looking out for the first temple they came across as they journeyed toward their goal.

5. HERACLES

Elissa, Teris and Smeme had descended from the mountains and were crossing a vast grassy plain. There was the occasional clump of small hybrid fir trees among the grass. In the distance, in every direction, they could see the tops of hills and mountains surrounding the plain. Walking was easier on the gravelly track, though a little monotonous.

Smeme offered to make the journey more interesting by telling stories he had heard, on his travels, about the nature of the Gods. Elissa and Teris accepted and Smeme spoke as they walked.

"Let me tell you the story of Arachne," Smeme began. "Everyone knows that the Gods are powerful and that we humans should always be humble and obedient before them. Yet, in ancient times, there was a beautiful woman called Arachne who had different ideas. Arachne was an expert at the loom and could weave the most intricate and wondrous designs into the cloth. Everyone who saw them found her creations enchanting and bewitching: it was as if they had been woven in Olympus by the Gods themselves, not on Earth by a mere mortal woman.

"As her fame grew, Arachne became prouder and prouder of her legendary talent. She boasted that no human could create finer works than hers. In fact, she could weave better than the Gods, even than Athena, the patron deity of handicrafts and the loom.

"People were shocked by Arachne's arrogant claim. They called on her to withdraw her impious remark. But this only inspired Arachne to go further. She said that if Athena did not agree with her, she should come and prove herself in an unbiased contest of weaving.

"Athena heard the challenge and accepted it willingly. She joined Arachne and the two stood at their looms, weaving with fine threads of many colors, including some of pure gold.

"The skill of Athena was undeniable. She created a dazzling depiction of her dispute with Poseidon over who should be chosen as the deity of Athens. It showed Poseidon offering the people of Athens a saltwater spring, while Athena offered them the olive tree. Around the main scene were four smaller ones. These portrayed the inevitable results of maintaining hubris against the Gods. One was about King Haemus of Thrace and his wife, Queen

Rhodope. Haemus was vain and proud. He compared himself and his wife to the ruling Gods of heaven, Zeus and Hera. He even set up a cult to worship himself and his queen. Zeus and Hera were so angered by this disrespect that they came and turned both the king and queen into mountains. Athena's tapestry showed the moment that Zeus and Hera transformed the king into the Haemus Mons and the queen into the Rhodope Mountains.

"The second smaller image was related to Gerana, a queen of the Pygmies. Gerana was very beautiful but lacked common decency. She failed to respect the Gods and even boasted that she was more beautiful than Hera, the Queen of the Gods. Hera heard of this hubris and was outraged. She came to Gerana after the birth of her first child and caused her neck to stretch until she turned into a crane. The second scene showed this startling metamorphosis.

"The third image was about Antigone, a princess of Troy, who dared to compare herself with the mighty Hera. Hera befittingly punished her arrogance by transforming her into a silly, chattering stork.

"The fourth image related to Myrrha, the daughter of King Cinyras of Cyprus. Her mother, Queen Cenchries, had boasted that Myrrha was more beautiful than Aphrodite. Aphrodite took revenge for this hubris by compelling Myrrha to trick her father into lying with her. When the king found out that he had been deceived, he wanted to kill Myrrha, but she fled the palace. The king pursued her for nine months. Heavily pregnant and realizing that she could never get away, Myrrha begged the Gods to help her. To hide her from her father, the Gods turned her into a myrrh tree. The tree also gave forth a baby, which grew to be the handsome youth, Adonis. The tapestry represented Myrrha at the moment she was transformed into a tree.

"To complete her tapestry, Athena wove elegant representations of olive wreaths, based on the tree she gave to Athens, around its edges.

"Arachne's tapestry was intricate, exquisitely detailed, and flawless. The intense colors ensnared the viewer's eyes and drew them from scene to scene. But what scenes! Arachne had carefully woven vibrant images of the less praiseworthy actions of the Gods. There were several of Zeus transforming himself into various animals and other forms so he could seduce different women. He was also shown engaging in multiple secret affairs with mortal women. The pictures were too shocking for a pious person to view, yet the eye was drawn back to them, again and again.

"Athena seized Arachne's tapestry and examined it closely. She studied every part but could not find a single thread out of place. The work was perfect. But such hubris in openly ridiculing the Gods, especially her own father, Zeus, could not be tolerated! She angrily tore the tapestry to pieces. Still in a rage, Athena turned to Arachne.

"'Since you have used your loom to mock the Gods, you and all your descendants shall hang from threads and be forced to weave for the rest of your lives!' Athena decreed.

"Athena then transformed the arrogant Arachne into a spider, hanging from its web."

"That was great, Smeme!" said Elissa. "I have heard that story before, but I loved your version!"

"Thank you," Smeme bowed as he walked.

"Yes, well told, Smeme," Teris agreed.

"What do you think the story means?" Smeme asked.

"I think it means that we should honor the Gods, such as Athena, and show them their due respect," Elissa replied. "But even though we want to do that, to honor their will, we have to admit that we do not always know what it really is," she added.

"That is very true, Elissa," Teris said.

"Yes, we do not always know what they want," Smeme concurred.

"That reminds me," Teris said. "When we were in Delphi, I saw some sayings on the forecourt wall of the temple of Apollo."

"What did you see?" asked Elissa.

"In the middle of the wall was written 'Know Thyself,'" Teris replied. "On the left was 'Nothing Too Much,' and on the right 'In a Pledge Ruin is Present.' Know Thyself is pretty obvious good advice, but I didn't get a chance to think about the other two."

"How does anyone know themselves?" Elissa shook her head. "I don't think I know that much about myself."

"But it's like you should know what you can achieve before you set out to do it," Teris said. "That way you would not attempt the impossible."

"Like my quest!" Elissa laughed.

Teris frowned. "I am not sure that is the same," he said.

"When you know yourself, what is it that you would know?" Smeme pondered. "I have seen that saying before. It is quite a good one, and very appropriate for the Oracle at Delphi. Very mysterious. It gets you going."

"Yes?" said Teris. He looked thoughtful.

"Well, I am not sure where it would lead," Elissa said. "Maybe you would find out who you are, but maybe you would only find out who you had been, not who you could be!"

"Who you could be? Yes, that is not always known by the person you are today," Smeme nodded.

"But if you knew that you couldn't achieve something, then how could you set out to do it?" Teris muttered to himself. "Except that maybe you could do it anyway! You are right, Elissa," he said more loudly.

"I am not so sure, but thanks anyway, Teris!" Elissa replied.

"What about 'Nothing Too Much'? What does that mean to you?" Smeme asked.

"What do you think, Elissa?" Teris invited.

"Me? I think that too much of anything is bad. Like when you eat too much. It is not good for you," Elissa said.

"Yes, that makes sense," Teris agreed.

"What about humility before the Gods? Could you have too much of that?" Smeme questioned.

"No. You couldn't," Elissa said.

Teris didn't speak.

"So, something could be 'Never Too Much,'" Smeme observed.

"Yes, I think so," Elissa said.

"But we still don't know everything that they want," Teris added.

"Indeed. Let's hope we can find out!" Smeme said, shaking his head.

"And the last one? What was that again?" Elissa asked.

"'In a Pledge Ruin is Present,'" Teris answered.

"That seems obvious!" Smeme said. "We should always be careful when we make a pledge, that it doesn't ruin us."

"True," Teris agreed. "That is the responsible and mature thing to do."

"Unless it is to someone you love," Elissa said. "Then you should keep your pledge no matter what it does to you."

"Yes, Elissa. You are right again," Teris said.

"Not a perfect score! But I'm doing all right!" Elissa joked.

They all laughed together.

"I think we've taken care of those sayings," Smeme said.

"Yes, it looks like it, Smeme," Teris agreed.

The three walked silently along the track.

"Smeme," Elissa said after a while, "do you have any other interesting stories about the Gods that you could tell? Maybe we could learn something from them."

"Yes, of course," Smeme replied. "Good idea. Would you like to hear about Heracles?"

Elissa and Teris nodded enthusiastically.

"Very well. As you know, Heracles was the son of Zeus, the Ruler of the Gods. Zeus had fallen in love with a beautiful mortal woman named Alcmene. Zeus transformed himself into the appearance of Alcmene's husband, Amphitryon, who was away at war. He then convinced Alcmene that he was her husband by telling her about his recent war victories. They lay together and Heracles was conceived. Alcmene's husband returned home later that same night, after Zeus had secretly left, and the twin brother of Heracles was conceived, Iphicles. It was only later that Alcmene discovered that the father of Heracles was not her husband.

"Hera, the Queen of Heaven, found out about Zeus's infidelity with Alcmene and became extremely jealous. She was especially upset because she had been unable to have any children with her husband, Zeus. She resolved to oppose Heracles.

"Nine months later, knowing that Alcmene was ready to give birth, and pretending to know nothing about her husband's infidelity, Hera persuaded Zeus to swear an oath that the next male child to be born of the House of Perseus would become the High King. Zeus easily agreed, as he knew that Heracles was about to be born to Alcmene, who was the granddaughter of the great hero, Perseus. But Hera had a trick in store.

"Hera went to the goddess Eileithyia, who looked after childbirth, and ordered her to delay the birth of Heracles and Iphicles. Hera then went and arranged the premature birth of Eurystheus, who was also a descendant of Perseus. Thanks to Hera's interventions, Eurystheus was born first and became the High King instead of Heracles. In adult life, Heracles was forced to serve his cousin, the sickly, weak King Eurystheus.

"Hera did not stop at this. When Heracles was still a baby, she sent two venomous snakes to kill him. The baby caught the snakes by their necks and dispatched them, laughing the whole time because he thought it was just a game. Hera set other traps for the young Heracles during his early years, but he remained unharmed and undefeated. She decided to wait for a better opportunity to exact her revenge.

"Heracles grew to be a fine young man, who was skilled in many of the physical arts, including archery, kopis fighting, wrestling and boxing. At the age of eighteen, Heracles heard that a lion was killing the sheep which belonged to his father, and also those owned by King Thespius of Thespiae. He hunted the lion for fifty days and finally caught it and wrestled it to death. From that time on, he wore the lion's skin as a cloak and its scalp as a helmet.

"On the way back from killing the lion, Heracles encountered the enemies of Thebes, who had come to collect the annual tribute for the king of the Minyans. Heracles fiercely punished them and sent them home. The Minyan king got his army together and marched against Thebes, but Heracles fought and killed him. Heracles then arranged for the Minyans to pay double the tribute to the Thebans.

"King Creon of Thebes was very grateful to Heracles and gave his eldest daughter, Megara, to him in marriage. Heracles and Megara were very happy together and had many children. Hera saw her chance to strike back at Heracles. She cast a spell on him that drove him completely mad. Heracles raged and went on a killing spree, slaughtering his beloved wife and children. Hera then completed her attack by returning Heracles to sanity, allowing him to see the destruction he had wreaked with his own hands.

"Heracles was devastated by the vision of his murdered family. He wept and tore at his hair. No one could console him. Aware of his terrible crime, Heracles traveled to the Oracle of Apollo at Delphi and sought instruction on how to make amends. The Pythia told Heracles that he would have to perform ten tasks set by his cousin, the High King Eurystheus. If he achieved the tasks, he would be forgiven his crimes and would also be granted immortality.

"Heracles went to Eurystheus and was assigned his first task: kill and bring to him an invulnerable lion that was ravaging the territory of Nemea. Heracles traveled to Nemea and hunted the lion. When he found it he shot arrows at it, but they just bounced off its armored skin. He also tried hitting it with his club, but that had no effect. Realizing that no weapon could penetrate its hide, Heracles trapped the lion in its cave and grasped it in his mighty arms, choking it to death. He then lifted its carcass onto his shoulders and carried it back to King Eurystheus. Eurystheus gave Heracles his second task, warning that each one would get harder and harder. To complete this task, Heracles had to kill the Lernaean Hydra.

"The Hydra was a monster that Hera herself had raised. She had reared it for only one purpose: to kill Heracles. The massive serpent had nine horrific heads. Heracles shot flaming arrows into the Hydra's lair, which was located in a deep cave near the swamp adjoining Lake Lerna. The Hydra emerged from its cave and launched itself at Heracles, who proceeded to smash off each of its heads with his heavy club. But each time he smashed off a head, two more grew in its place. Realizing that he could not kill the Hydra this way, Heracles called for his nephew and squire, Iolaus, to come and help him. Iolaus made some torches and burnt each neck after Heracles had smashed off a head, stopping them from growing. Soon there was only one head left: the immortal one. Heracles chopped this off, buried it, and placed a giant rock on top of it. It was trapped, still alive and writhing, in the ground under the rock. Finally, with the thought that it may be of some use in the future, Heracles dipped his arrowheads in the poisonous blood of the slain Hydra.

"When Heracles returned to King Eurystheus and described what he had done, the king said that it could not be counted as one of his ten tasks as Iolaus had assisted him. Heracles must perform the tasks on his own. Heracles humbly accepted Eurystheus's ruling.

"For the next task, Eurystheus commanded Heracles to fetch him, alive, the Hind of Ceryneia. This deer had golden antlers, similar in shape to those of a stag, and bronze hooves. It was sacred to the goddess Artemis, which meant that it could not be harmed in any way. How could Heracles capture it and bring it to Eurystheus without hurting it?

"Heracles hunted the deer for one whole year, but it was very elusive and kept escaping him. Eventually, the deer tired of the chase and looked for a place to rest on the Artemisius mountain. It went to the edge of the Ladon River and was about to swim across when Heracles spotted it. Heracles was tired of chasing the deer for so long and, in spite of it being sacred to Artemis, wounded it with an arrow. He captured the injured deer and carried it on his shoulders toward Tiryns.

"As Heracles hurried along with his catch, he encountered Artemis and Apollo blocking the path. Artemis was very angry with Heracles. She stepped forward to take her sacred hind from him and was sure to punish him severely for his attempt to kill it, but Heracles explained that he had no choice but to obey the oracle of her brother, Apollo, and perform all the tasks that King Eurystheus assigned him. This was the only way that he could pay due penance for his earlier crimes. Apollo confirmed that this was the case. Hearing her brother's confirmation, and seeing that Heracles had been honest and respectful toward her, caused Artemis to soften her anger. She took the deer from Heracles and healed its wound. So he could complete his task, Artemis gave Heracles permission for him to take it alive to King Eurystheus.

"Hearing that Eurystheus intended to keep the hind in his animal collection, Heracles devised a way to protect it without breaking his promise to the king. He called to Eurystheus to come out and accept the hind into his own hand, as was only fitting for such a magnificent creature. Eurystheus agreed and reached out his hand to take the hind, but Heracles released his grip just before the king touched it. The hind immediately fled at high speed back to the wilderness, to live safely under the protection of its divine mistress, Artemis. Thus, Heracles fulfilled his promise to the king while simultaneously honoring the Goddess who had helped him.

"The next task assigned to Heracles was to capture the wild boar of Mount Erymanthus and bring it, still alive, to the king."

Elissa shuddered at the thought of that vicious wild boar.

"This huge shaggy boar would set out daily from its mountain lair and harass the people and animals in the nearby region of Psophis in western Arcadia. Heracles soon found the wild boar. With loud shouts, he drove it out from the trees and into heavy snow. The boar became weakened by its struggles through the snow, enabling Heracles to snare it with a noose. He then lifted it onto his left shoulder and carried it to Mycenae. Such was his immense strength!

"King Eurystheus was petrified by the sight of Heracles carrying the huge live boar in his arms and hid in a large bronze jar. He had previously arranged for the jar to be brought and partly buried in the ground so he could escape from Heracles if needed. Eventually, he emerged from the jar and gave Heracles his next task. The king ordered Heracles to clean out the stables of King Augeas, and this had to be done in one single day, without assistance from any other person.

"Heracles knew that this would be no easy task, even for someone of his massive strength, because the stables contained a huge amount of dung that had built up over many years from the thousands of oxen and goats that King Augeas owned. Heracles was also conscious that this task was insulting to someone of his background.

"King Augeas was amazed when Heracles came to him and proposed to cleanse his stables in one day. He offered the hero one-tenth of his best cattle as a reward, if he could accomplish the task.

"Heracles dug ditches from two nearby rivers, Alpheus and Peneus, to the stables. The water rushed down the ditches and through the stables, cleaning out all the dung in one day. Augeas was amazed by Heracles' accomplishment but refused to award him the cattle he had earned, saying that he had used trickery rather than hard labor to get the result. Augeas's eldest son, Phyleus, objected to the mistreatment of Heracles. For this, Augeas banished Phyleus from his land.

"Heracles was angered by Augeas's refusal to pay and waged war against him. After much fighting, Heracles and his army conquered the land of King Augeas and slew him in battle. Heracles gave the land to Phyleus to rule. Phyleus awarded Heracles the cattle that were owed to him.

"Heracles took his payment and went back to King Eurystheus to tell him what he had done.

"Eurystheus was not impressed. He told Heracles that his achievement did not count as he had been paid for his work. He would have to complete another task in place of the stable cleaning. Since he liked large groups of animals so much, his next task would be to chase away a huge flock of birds that had gathered at a lake near the town of Stymphalos.

"Heracles went to the lake and saw the multitude of birds swimming on its surface. He tried waving his arms and shouting at the birds but they just flew into the air briefly and then returned to the water. Heracles shot some arrows at them, but to little effect. He had to think.

"Heracles came up with the idea of making a bronze crotalum. He prepared the metal in a fire and fashioned it into the device. Taking his newly-made crotalum to a high point near the lake, he clapped it together hard and long, making a terrible din. The birds were disturbed by the infernal clattering and flew away en masse, never to be seen in the area again.

"Heracles returned to Eurystheus and reported his success.

"Heracles' next task was a simple one for a person of his towering strength. But maybe you would like to take a break from all these stories now?" Smeme suggested.

"Let's just have a snack and then you can continue when we are walking again," Elissa proposed.

"Great!" said Smeme.

The three stopped for a short rest and then resumed their long journey.

"What happened to Heracles next, Smeme?" Elissa prompted.

"Heracles had to capture a large crazed bull that was terrorizing the island of Crete. He sailed to Crete and went in pursuit of the bull.

"Now, this bull was a special one that Minos, the king of Crete, should have sacrificed to the God of the sea, Poseidon. Each year, King Minos sacrificed the most attractive bull in his herds to Poseidon, but one year he found the bull so beautiful that he did not want to sacrifice it. He sacrificed an inferior bull instead. This angered Poseidon, who responded by making the bull go on a frenzied rampage all over Crete. He also made King Minos's wife, Pasiphae, fall in love with the bull, resulting in the birth of the half-human, half-bull monster, the Minotaur. King Minos trapped this beast in the Labyrinth, a complex series of winding passageways built underneath his royal palace. Every year he had to feed it prisoners from Athens, as you will have heard.

"Heracles traveled to Crete and, grabbing it by its horns, wrestled the crazed bull to the ground. He took it back to Mycenae on his ship and delivered it to King Eurystheus. Eurystheus set the bull free. It wandered far, finally arriving at Marathon, where it attacked the local people. Later, our great Athenian hero, Theseus, sacrificed it to Apollo. Theseus also went to Crete. He navigated to the center of the Labyrinth and killed the Minotaur, removing its evil from the world. But that's another story!

"Heracles was ready for his eighth task. Eurystheus asked Heracles to bring him the man-eating mares of Diomedes, king of the Bistones.

"Heracles got together a band of volunteers and sailed to Bistonia. They snuck into the stables and overpowered the grooms. They then drove the mares to the sea, ready to load onto their ship, but the Bistones realized what had happened and sent soldiers to recover the mares. Heracles wanted to go and fight the soldiers, so he left the mares under the care of a youth called Abderus.

"Heracles went with his volunteers to do battle with the soldiers. In the meantime, the mares proved too strong for Abderus to hold. They pulled him from his feet and dragged him across the stony ground, bouncing him over the rocks until he was dead.

"Heracles and his team defeated the soldiers. Heracles killed King Diomedes in the battle. The surviving soldiers fled. Heracles returned to find Abderus dead. He resolved to honor Abderus's courage by founding a new city in his name: Abdera. Heracles and his team recaptured the mares and took them back to Eurystheus on their ship.

"The weak king, Eurystheus, set the mares free. They wandered around Mycenae until they eventually arrived at Mount Olympus, where they were killed and eaten by the wild beasts of the area.

"Heracles was up to his ninth labor now. For this one, Eurystheus commanded Heracles to bring him the belt of Hippolyte, the queen of the Amazons, as his daughter, Admete, wanted it for herself.

"The Amazons, though all female, were great warriors. If they ever gave birth, they only kept the females, teaching them the martial arts that they knew.

"Ares had awarded Queen Hippolyte his own war-belt in recognition of her superior warrior spirit. She wore it proudly across her chest.

"Heracles gathered his friends together and sailed with them to the land of the Amazons. They entered the harbor and disembarked. Queen Hippolyte came to Heracles and asked him his business there. Heracles openly explained his assignment. Hippolyte was impressed by his honesty and promised to give him her belt to take back to Eurystheus.

"Hera heard the promise and determined to block Heracles from success. She disguised herself as an Amazon woman and went up and down the town saying that the strangers had come to abduct their queen. The Amazonians grabbed their weapons and came thundering down to the harbor on their horses. When Heracles saw the armed horde charging toward his party he suspected Hippolyte of setting a trap for them. He killed Hippolyte, took her belt, and joined his team in fighting off the Amazons. The party then reboarded their ship and sailed back to Mycenae, stopping briefly at Troy on the way so that they could replenish their supplies.

"In Mycenae, Heracles gave the belt of Hippolyte to King Eurystheus.

"Still, there was more for Heracles to do! Eurystheus assigned him his tenth task: bring back the cattle of the monster Geryon.

"Geryon was a giant who had three heads, three bodies joined together at one waist, and three sets of legs below. He was a formidable warrior! He was born from Chrysaor, who sprang from the decapitated body of the Medusa after Perseus had beheaded her, and Callirrhoe, the daughter of the Titans, Oceanus and Tethys. Geryon lived on the remote island of Erytheia, in the far west Mediterranean. There he kept a herd of magnificent crimson-colored cattle. The cattle were herded by Eurytion and protected by Orthrus, a hound that had two heads and was the brother of the three-headed Cerberus, that ferocious canine that guards the gates of the underworld!

"The journey was long. Heracles left Mycenae and walked west across all of Europe, then southward until he came to the westernmost edge of the Mediterranean, where you could cross to Libya. Needless to say, he encountered various wild beasts on the way, easily killing any that were foolhardy enough to attack him!

"At the crossing to Libya, he decided to build a memorial to honor his long journey, so he split a mountain in two, placing one half in Europe and the other in Libya. These have been known as the Pillars of Heracles to this day. The space left by the mountain filled with water from the Mediterranean and is now the route that ships can take to leave our sea and voyage afar, to the great ocean at the end of the world.

"Heracles then started crossing the Libyan desert. He found the heat intolerable and got so angry that he pointed an arrow at Helios and stretched back his bow. The Titan sun god was surprised by this daring and awarded Heracles a huge golden goblet in recognition of his courage. Heracles carried the goblet to the sea and used it to sail to the island of Erytheia.

"As Heracles landed on the island, the terrifying two-headed dog, Orthrus, confronted him. Heracles took his trusty club and killed the hound with one massive blow. The cowherd, Eurytion, came running up to help the dog, but Heracles also hit him with his club, quickly dispatching him. Geryon, hearing all the noise, hurriedly put on his three helmets, grabbed his three shields and three spears, and raced toward Heracles. Heracles took up his bow and shot an arrow that had been dipped in the blood of the Lernaean Hydra. The arrow struck so hard that it went through one of Geryon's foreheads. Geryon's three heads fell lifelessly to their sides as his three giant bodies collapsed onto the ground.

"Heracles was now free to herd the fine crimson cattle back to Eurystheus – an epic journey! Heracles loaded the cattle into the golden goblet and sailed it back to the border of Europe and Libya. He disembarked the cattle and returned the goblet to Helios. He then drove the cattle toward Mycenae. He fought off anyone who tried to steal the cattle and eventually got near to home. But Hera was angered by Heracles' success and sent a cloud of gadflies to bite the cattle and irritate them, causing them to scatter. The cattle ran far and wide. Heracles could only gather some of the herd back together, leaving the rest to go wild. Heracles blamed the river Strymon for the gadflies and punished it by filling it with rocks. Finally, Heracles got the cattle to King Eurystheus. The king thought it fit to sacrifice all the cattle to Hera. Poor Heracles!

"Heracles had now performed ten tasks for his penance, over more than eight years, but Eurystheus still had two more tasks for him to perform. The first of these was to bring him the golden apples that Gaia had given as a wedding gift to Zeus and Hera.

"The golden apples were in a garden at the northernmost edge of the world. They were guarded by an immortal hundred-headed dragon, Ladon, and by four nymphs called the Hesperides, who were the daughters of the Titan, Atlas.

"Heracles set off in search of the garden, as no mortal knew where it was. He traveled through many lands. One time he was stopped by Cycnus, the son of Ares, and challenged to a fight. Heracles was doing well, but the fight was broken up by a thunderbolt – maybe that came from Zeus. In any case, he had to continue on his way without completing the challenge. Heracles journeyed on to Illyria. There he grabbed the sea-god Nereus, the old man of the sea, because the ancient god knew the secret of where the garden was located. Nereus transformed himself into multiple creatures in Heracles' arms, but this did not frighten Heracles. Whatever Nereus changed into, Heracles kept holding him tight. Nereus had no choice but to reveal the garden's location. After that, Heracles let him go.

"Heracles went via Libya in the direction of the secret garden, but was stopped by Antaeus, a son of Poseidon. Antaeus fought everyone who came his way, and challenged Heracles to a wrestling match to the death. Antaeus had killed so many passing warriors that he had been able to build a hideous temple out of their skulls. Heracles knew that Antaeus drew his formidable power from the earth, as it was his mother, Gaia, so he grasped Antaeus in his arms and lifted him off the ground, breaking the source of his strength. Heracles then crushed him to death in a powerful hold.

"Heracles continued on his way, arriving in Egypt, but had the misfortune of running into Busiris and his soldiers. Busiris was a son of Poseidon, like Antaeus, and was also an Egyptian king. He and his men seized Heracles and took him to their altar to be sacrificed to Zeus, as the king had been told that for the country's famine to end, he would have to make an annual human offering of a foreigner to the King of the Gods. At the precise moment when Heracles was to be executed, he suddenly broke his bonds and jumped from the altar, killing Busiris and his son before fleeing.

"As Heracles journeyed north, he passed Mount Caucasus. There, the great Titan Prometheus had been chained. For the crime of disobeying Zeus by giving the gift of fire to humans, Prometheus had been sentenced to a terrible punishment. Every day, a gigantic eagle came and ate Prometheus's liver, pecking it out of his living body. After the eagle left, the liver grew back, setting Prometheus up for another day of torture. This had been happening for a great many years.

"Heracles took pity on Prometheus and determined to rescue him. He lay in wait for the giant eagle and shot it with one of his poisoned arrows. He then tore Prometheus's chains apart with his bare hands.

"Prometheus was very grateful. In return for his liberation, he told Heracles how to get the golden apples of Hera. Rather than try to enter the secret garden by himself, Heracles should instead send Atlas to get them.

"Heracles thanked Prometheus and set off to find Atlas. Atlas was busy with the tiring task of holding up the earth and the sky on his mighty shoulders. Heracles asked Atlas if, in return for taking over his heavy burden for a while, he would go and get the golden apples for him. Atlas happily agreed and passed the earth and sky to Heracles. Heracles strained under the weight but, thanks to his unprecedented strength, was able to hold up the enormous load. After some days, Atlas returned with the apples. Heracles got ready to hand back the world, but Atlas asked him to keep holding it up for a little while longer, as Atlas intended to take the apples to Eurystheus himself.

"Heracles was suspicious of Atlas's motives. Would he really return to take back the heavy burden that Zeus had sentenced him to hold for all eternity? Heracles thought fast. He told Atlas that he agreed with the plan, but asked him if he could please take the earth and sky for a moment so he could put some padding on his shoulders, as they were aching from the weight. Atlas kindly assented and put the golden apples on the ground. He then took the earth and sky from Heracles.

"Heracles picked up the apples and quickly ran away, leaving Atlas with his ancient load. Heracles returned to Mycenae and gave the golden apples to King Eurystheus. Eurystheus was annoyed that yet another impossible task had been completed by Heracles. Realizing that the apples could not be kept by any mortal, Eurystheus bestowed them on

Heracles. Heracles secretly took the apples to a temple of Athena and placed them inside, praying that they be returned to their hidden garden. The Goddess Athena heard the prayer and came and took the golden apples back to the garden before any harm could come to her favorite mortal, Heracles.

"Eurystheus was beside himself with frustration. He could not get over the fact that Heracles had been able to complete so many obviously impossible tasks. He decided to impose one that was completely beyond human achievability: Heracles would have to capture the three-headed dog that guarded the underworld and bring it back to him… and, the ferocious beast would have to be presented completely unharmed! Heracles stoically accepted the challenge.

"To prepare himself for the realm of the dead, Heracles traveled to the sanctuary of Eleusis and sought initiation into the Eleusinian Mysteries. After he had completed the secret sacred rites, Heracles sought out Hermes to guide him into the underworld.

"Hermes took Heracles down into the world ruled by Hades, where all those who are no longer living reside. As Heracles entered the underworld, he was confronted by the terrifying, snake-haired Gorgon, Medusa. He drew his kopis to fight the monster, but Hermes said not to bother: it was just an empty phantom, she was no longer alive. Heracles continued deeper into the underworld. He came across two of his friends, Theseus and Pirithous. Each was stuck in a chair and could not move. The pair held out their hands to Heracles as if begging him to set them free. With his great strength, Heracles managed to wrench Theseus loose from his chair. He then turned to help Pirithous, but the ground began to shake violently and, not wanting to anger Hades, Heracles ceased the attempt. Heracles took Theseus with him and sought out Hades' underground palace.

"At the palace, Heracles asked the great God's permission to take his ferocious guard dog, Cerberus, with him. Hades agreed to this request, but on the condition that Heracles did not use any weapons to capture the three-headed hound. Heracles advanced on the savage, slavering beast, with its tail of a serpent and mane made from the heads of all sorts of snakes, and grabbed its head with his sinewy arms. The dog struggled violently, its serpent tail striking Heracles many times, but finding no way to free itself from Heracles' chokehold, the hound submitted to its new master. Taking Theseus with him, Heracles led Cerberus out of the underworld and across the land of the living to King Eurystheus.

"As soon as Eurystheus saw Heracles arriving with Cerberus, he fled and hid in his giant bronze jar. From inside the jar, he ordered Heracles to return the horrendous three-headed hound to Hades immediately. Heracles was happy to comply.

"Heracles had successfully completed all his labors and was freed from the guilt of his terrible crime. He was no longer obliged to his cousin, the weak King Eurystheus, and was allowed to live however he pleased.

"As you may be aware, Heracles had to wait some years before Apollo's promise of immortality was granted. He now lives for eternity in Olympus," Smeme concluded.

"That was an amazing story!" Elissa said admiringly.

"Some parts were a little different to what I have heard before," Teris observed.

"Is that so?" Smeme said. "It depends which poet you were listening to. Each one had a different view!"

"I mostly heard about it in the gymnasium," Teris admitted.

"But Heracles would know what happened!" Elissa offered. "Even if it was so long ago."

"I expect he would," Smeme replied. "You could ask him when you get to Olympus."

"I don't think I will bother anyone with that," Elissa replied. "Anyway, we have to get there first!"

"Indeed," Smeme said. "But, for now, let's have lunch!"

Everyone agreed and they stopped to have a break and a meal.

While they were eating, Smeme asked his companions what they might learn from the story of Heracles, especially about the nature of the Gods.

"What do *you* think it meant, Smeme?" Elissa asked.

"The obvious lesson is that we can anger the Gods just by the circumstances of our birth," Smeme replied. "We don't have to have done anything at all: it was done to us."

"Yes, but Heracles was ultimately accepted into Olympus and made immortal," Elissa objected. "It seems that he eventually earned the Gods' respect by faithfully completing the twelve labors that were assigned to him."

"I think you are right that Heracles earned their respect through his heroism and honor, Elissa," Smeme concurred.

"I agree," Teris said. "We must struggle to do what is right, no matter how difficult it is for us."

Smeme looked surprised.

"That is not quite what I meant, young warrior," Smeme said, "but I must admit that it is completely true."

Teris nodded.

"But what do these stories really tell us about the nature of the Gods?" Elissa wondered. "Yes, we may have to fear their immense powers, obviously, and then what? I think we are missing something that would help us to answer this riddle."

Elissa turned to Smeme.

"Smeme, do you know any story that would answer the question of why we have to follow the Gods' wills or laws, by doing what is right, no matter how difficult it will be for us? In your travels, has such a thing been told to you?"

Smeme considered.

"I think I have something," Smeme replied. "I will tell you as we walk."

The team finished eating and resumed their journey. Elissa and Teris listened to Smeme as they walked.

"This is the story of the fateful love of Orpheus and Eurydice," Smeme began. "Orpheus was the most skilled lyre player in the entire world. When he played, he could charm even rocks and rivers. No one was immune to the beauty of his music.

"Orpheus fell in love with the lovely wood nymph, Eurydice. He wooed her with his lyre and enchanting voice. Unfortunately, their happy time together was brief, as shortly after their wedding, Eurydice was bitten by a viper and died. Orpheus was heartbroken and went to search for Eurydice in the underworld. First, he encountered the ferocious three-headed dog, Cerberus, which, as you know, guards the gates to the underworld. He soothed it with gentle music and kept playing until the hound fell asleep. Orpheus then met the ruler of the underworld, Hades, and his wife, Persephone. Hades and Persephone were so moved by Orpheus's beautiful song that they agreed to let Eurydice leave the underworld and live again on earth, but there was one condition: Eurydice would have to follow Orpheus while she was walking out to the light from the darkness of the underworld and Orpheus must not turn and look at her until she was fully out in the light of day. Orpheus gladly accepted the condition and led his silent, expressionless wife across the underworld and then uphill toward the land of the living. As he was walking up the slope, Orpheus began to have doubts. Maybe the Gods were making fun of him. He could not hear Eurydice's footsteps behind him: perhaps she was not really there. Orpheus continued to walk, but his doubts gnawed at him and finally overwhelmed him. Only a few steps from the exit of the under-world, he looked back to check if his wife was genuinely behind him. Eurydice was indeed there, but as a shade that could only become flesh again in the light of day. As Orpheus's gaze fell on her, Eurydice's shade fell backward into the darkness of the underworld, now trapped there forever."

Elissa was deeply moved by the story.

"Smeme, how does this tragic story help us to answer the question of why we have to follow the Gods' wills or laws? Was Orpheus failing to do what was right, no matter how difficult it was for him?" Elissa asked.

"I think this story shows that Orpheus failed to follow a God's will and that this must lead to tragedy," Smeme replied. "The same lesson must apply to following all the Gods and their instruc-tions."

"I see," Elissa murmured, biting her lip.

Teris looked thoughtful but said nothing.

The three walked in silence for a while.

6. ERIS

The sun was getting low in the sky when the team came across a village on the grassy plain. They located the inn and went inside to rest for the night. After their evening meal, Elissa asked the innkeeper where the nearest temple was. He replied that the village was small and only had a simple outdoor altar for making offerings. Elissa thanked him and went to her room to sleep, realizing that in this remote region it might be some time before she found a temple where she could ask the Gods her question.

As she slept, Elissa dreamed about Arachne, Heracles and Orpheus. Orpheus was playing his lyre and singing a beautiful song. He gazed at Elissa as he sang, for this was a song of his love for her. Suddenly, Heracles came into the room and grabbed

Orpheus. He shook the hapless musician. "Elissa is mine!" Heracles shouted. Trapped in the hero's mighty grip, Orpheus passed out and fell to the floor. Heracles turned to Elissa and was about to stride across the room to her when a giant female spider raced over the floor and bound him in its web. The web was multicolored. Elissa saw that the web was woven like a tapestry. As the spider wrapped more web around the struggling Heracles, the design became apparent. There were beautiful depictions of the Gods going about their work. One was of Zeus changing into the husband of Alcmene and leading her to her bed. Another was of Athena weaving a tapestry of her own. It was strange to see Heracles being bound in a spiderweb tapestry that included an image of the day of his own conception! And what would Athena think of seeing a representation of herself weaving at her loom in a web created by the very person whom she had turned into a spider in the first place, Arachne!

Athena abruptly appeared. This frightened the giant Arachne spider, which fled over the floor, clambered up the wall, and disappeared through the open window. Athena drew her knife and cut into the web tapestry, setting Heracles free. Athena promptly vanished in a mist. Heracles pulled the web open and leaped out from its confines. He spied Elissa. He resumed his journey toward her, but the room vanished and Heracles found himself at the entrance to the underground realm of Hades, facing the three-headed hound, Cerberus, all over again. Heracles approached the menacing hound and went to grasp it in his bare arms when beautiful music rang forth. It was coming from the lyre of Orpheus. Orpheus began to sing a calming lullaby, causing Cerberus to stop his attack and lie down to sleep. Heracles whispered his thanks to Orpheus. He suggested that, as Orpheus was now his friend, they could enter the underworld and rescue Elissa together. Orpheus agreed, but with a sad voice, as he was remembering the loss of his beautiful wife, Eurydice.

Elissa was being held hostage by the Queen of the Amazons, who was a multi-headed beast. Each of her nine heads breathed fire. Around the Queen were savage horses that ate human flesh. They dragged a poor boy around until he was dead and then went to eat him, but Heracles' sailors frightened them away. They buried the boy and from his grave grew a giant wild boar that had three heads, three bodies and three sets of legs. The boar kept attractive crimson-colored cattle on an island in the underworld, far away from Mycenae. Heracles traveled there in a golden goblet, but had to take the world from the shoulders of Orpheus so his new friend could rest and play his lyre. The music lulled Hades to sleep, allowing Orpheus to take the golden apples of Hera and eat them. Hera was angered by this theft and decided to drive Heracles mad for bringing his friend into the underworld, where the secret garden of the apples lay. Heracles threw the world onto the shoulders of Atlas and turned to attack his friend Orpheus, but Orpheus sang and played beautiful music secretly written by Athena. The soothing notes made Heracles sane again.

Heracles shook his friend's hand and thanked him. They continued on their quest to rescue Elissa.

A giant Sphinx was asking Elissa a question. If Elissa could answer she would be freed from the Queen of the Amazons. "What goes around when it's down, and up when it's round?" the Sphinx asked, with a menacing expression. Elissa had no idea and asked Smeme, but he had turned into a huge lion and could not speak. Teris had an answer: "Arachne's hubris." The Sphinx laughed and went to eat Teris, but a giant spider wrapped it in her tapestry web. She had come here after fleeing through the open window of the inn. The web had beautiful pictures of Elissa's journey woven into it. Elissa could make out the temple of Apollo at Delphi, the fight with the dragon, and other note-worthy scenes.

Meanwhile, Heracles and Orpheus had fought off a range of attackers, including various giants, to finally arrive at the inn. The inn was on top of Mount Olympus now. Zeus and the other Gods were amazed by the appearance of the inn but feared to go near it, as Phobos had taken a liking to it and stood on its roof, projecting an eerie green light all around him. The Harpies flew in the air above Phobos's head, ready to shriek and swoop down on anyone who approached their master and his prized country inn. King Eurystheus hid in a huge bronze jar to avoid the danger.

Heracles tore up the ground with his bare hands and directed two mighty rivers at the inn. The gushing water swept the inn off the mountain, cleaning it thoroughly as it carried it down to the land of its origin. The water subsided, leaving the inn standing in its small village, as if nothing had happened.

Elissa woke to find herself untouched and unmoved from the bed in her room. A pale beam of moonlight filtered through the window shutters. It was still night. She turned over and went back to sleep.

While Elissa slept, Smeme and Teris stayed up for a while in the main room of the inn. Teris was careful not to drink too much these days. He didn't want a repeat of his foolishness from earlier in the journey. A whimpering sound came from outside. Smeme went to investigate. As his eyes adjusted to the dim light, Smeme could make out an injured dog that was limping about the street, whining in pain. He felt sorry for the poor animal and went over to help it.

The dog looked up at Smeme pitifully. Smeme stepped forward to pat it but it limped off into the night. Smeme followed. The injured dog looked back to check that Smeme was pursuing and hobbled into the nearby forest.

"What's wrong, my poor friend?" Smeme called. He navigated carefully among the dark trees, seeking the injured animal.

The dog whimpered back at Smeme but kept going.

Smeme came into a clearing in the forest. The light from the moon was brighter here. Smeme could make out a beautiful, mature woman standing in the middle of the clearing. She saw Smeme emerging from among the trees and came toward him.

"Thank you for your concern about my poor pet, stranger," the woman said. "I am Eugenia. It is so rare to meet a man who cares for the animals of others."

Smeme smiled. "I am Smeme," he said. "I am a lover of all our animal friends."

"That is so," Eugenia said. "I could see that at once." She was now standing in front of Smeme.

Perhaps it was the moonlight, Smeme thought, but this woman was the most beautiful that he had ever seen. What a surprise to find a mature potential mate in a remote place like this at night! He imagined giving up his solitary roaming life and settling down happily with a kindred spirit at last.

"Where is your dog?" Smeme suddenly asked.

"She has gone off toward our home," Eugenia replied. "But what of you? Would you care to come with me for some refreshment?"

Smeme nodded in the dim light. Eugenia turned and started to lead him across the clearing.

"With an ugly beast like you?" a voice came from the trees.

Eugenia span around. Her eyes probed the darkness behind Smeme.

"Where are you?" Eugenia demanded.

"Wouldn't you like to know, you hideous deformity of ill-famed delusion!" the voice replied.

Smeme recognized the voice. He wondered what his friend was up to.

"Deformity! Why you…" Eugenia began, but was interrupted by her own scream. She shrieked like a Harpy as she was transformed from the beautiful into the grotesque. Her upright form twisted and turned until the nauseating sight of Empusa appeared, with her single donkey leg shod in a bronze sandal. Her malformed face scowled toward the trees, its sharp yellow teeth appearing from behind her pulled-back black lips.

Smeme became aware of the foul odor of Empusa's fetid breath enveloping him as she scanned the trees, looking for her accuser. He felt vomit rising in his throat.

"Did you come to eat my friend, you evil beast?" the voice taunted. "Now you are exposed in your deceit. Flee!" the voice commanded.

Empusa paused for a moment, her dark eyes staring into the shadows among the trees. But there was nothing she could do. She had been seen. Her true form was unmasked. She turned and fled, hopping rapidly across the clearing and into the forest on the other side, disappearing from view.

Teris stepped out from behind the trees.

"Are you all right, dear friend?" Teris asked, grasping Smeme's shoulder.

"Only thanks to you!" Smeme replied, taking Teris's hand and shaking it vigorously.

Teris laughed. "I am glad I followed you!"

"Me too!" Smeme said, joining in the laughter.

"How did you know it was Empusa?" Smeme asked.

"I didn't. But I didn't want to take any chances," Teris replied. "When I saw you following that dog, I thought I had better keep an eye on you, just in case. When it turned into a woman I was sure that something was wrong!”

“It turned into a woman? I didn’t see that,” Smeme said.

“Yes. Then I thought it could be Empusa again, come to get revenge on you for last time,” Teris said.

“I’m surprised she followed me this far. I must have really upset her!”

“It seems so,” Teris smiled. “So, I remembered your advice to slander her. The rest is history, as they say!”

“Indeed it is,” Smeme said. “Instead of *me* being history!” He laughed.

“You are still current,” Teris said. “History will have to keep waiting for you!”

Smeme and Teris laughed together again. The pair turned and walked back through the shadowy forest with their arms clasped around each other’s shoulders. They entered the inn, finished their drinks and went to their room to sleep. There had been enough adventure for one night.

The next day the three continued their long journey. They were still crossing the vast grassy plain which was surrounded by mountains. Life, for the few people who inhabited the plain, looked peaceful enough here, though a little harsh. The main occupation seemed to be raising goats, as the local grass was not nutritious enough for sheep. This was a very different world from her father's farm at home in Oe, Elissa thought.

While Elissa was walking and observing the landscape, Teris continued to scan the scene around them for danger. You never knew what might be coming to greet them next!

Teris moved closer to Smeme.

"Smeme, do you know that man in the agora in Athens who has been asking people a lot of questions?" Teris asked.

"Yes, I have heard about him," Smeme replied.

"So, what do you think when he asks questions about what is the genuine good life?" Teris asked.

"That is a difficult subject," Smeme said. "I am not sure that I could cover it successfully, in spite of all my years," he admitted.

"Yes, I believe that even the wise have had trouble answering that man!" Teris observed.

"I can imagine," Smeme agreed.

"Then, if we have so much trouble with these questions, how are we supposed to know what is the real good life? How can we know if it is the quest for Athlos, for example, or the faithful worship of the Gods, or what?" Teris asked.

"Indeed. Yes. How?" Smeme replied.

"How does anyone know anything about anything?" Teris complained. "That is what I would like to know!"

Smeme thought over his many experiences. Teris's style of questioning was new to him. He had heard men discussing a great number of things in his life, but never in this manner. He wondered how this reflected on all the things he had studied and thought about over the years.

"You know, that is very interesting, young man," Smeme said. "I have traveled far and wide, and had many experiences in my life, but I have never heard anyone questioning in quite the way that you do. Most of us think that we know what's what: that we know the answers already, as it were. But you have done something different.

"I find that I can no longer say what the answers to such questions might be. Listening to you, I have lost my confidence. Perhaps this is what that Socrates is talking about?" Smeme mused.

"It may be," Teris said. "I don't know, I have never met him. In any case, I have heard that he does not know the answers to these things himself!"

"At least, that is what he says," Smeme observed.

"Oh, I see. Good point," Teris nodded.

"But how can we mere mortals expect to understand the will of the Gods?" Smeme suddenly blurted out. "They and the Titans are the great beings who existed long before we men. They were the ones who created the universe and told us what to do... how to live. They gave us fire and taught us how to farm... how to make music... weave cloth, make pottery... all the skills! It was Athena herself who brought us the olive, so important to our lives. With all these things, how are we mortals to answer such questions as Socrates asks by ourselves?"

Teris considered Smeme's outburst. He could not think of an answer to these points either. Perhaps that questioning Athenian was some kind of great fool. Who else but a fool would dare to question the Gods? But, then, perhaps that is not what the Athenian meant?

"Maybe it would be better to leave these questions for later, Smeme," Teris suggested.

Smeme pondered.

"I think you are right, wise young man!" he suddenly said, cheerfully.

The pair raced to catch up with Elissa, who had been striding ahead of them, lost in thought herself. The party continued walking in silence, Teris and Smeme still looking around themselves, alert for any danger.

The three traveled for hours across the plain, finally reaching its northernmost edge at the base of some hills in the late afternoon. They made camp there for the night.

The morning came and the team continued their journey, slowly climbing the steep slopes of the hills. There were more trees here, mostly black pine, with some Bosnian pine and the occasional beech. In the more open areas the team also saw sporadic clusters of hybrid fir, which were shorter and bushier than those they had seen on the grassy plain. The three climbed silently, each engrossed in their own thoughts, but they also kept watch, alert to the dangers that may surround them, wondering if one would be that unclimbable object, whatever it may be!

Halfway up the hill, the trees opened into a small clearing. The area had been leveled. A magnificent white marble temple stood in the center of the clearing, its tall pillars supporting a colorful, elaborately decorated pediment. The grounds were filled with exquisite statues covered in gold.

Elissa, Teris and Smeme walked up to the front of the temple, looking for a priest or priestess in attendance. They searched around the outside of the temple but could not find anyone. Not wanting to enter uninvited, Teris went to the portico and called through the temple door: "Is anyone there?" There was a movement from far inside. After some time, a figure came forward. Teris stepped back into the temple grounds. A priestess ambled out of the temple chamber and stood in the portico.

"Yes?" the priestess said in an annoyed tone. "Was someone calling?"

The priestess was dressed in a fine multicolored peplos and had an intricate hairstyle replete with various jeweled gold pins.

"Sorry to trouble you, Mistress," Teris replied, "but we were hoping that we could make an offering here."

"An offering?" the priestess answered. "What do you mean? Only true believers can make offerings at this site."

"But we are true believers," Teris complained.

"Are you really?" the priestess retorted. "In what God?"

"In all the Gods, Mistress," Teris replied.

"You don't even know which God this temple is dedicated to!" the priestess scoffed. "Be on your way, the three of you. You are not true believers in my Goddess. I don't believe that you even follow any of the Gods. Begone!" She angrily waved the team away and then turned and went back into the temple.

Teris and Elissa stood dejected.

"Wait!" Smeme called to the departing figure.

The priestess turned back and stared at Smeme.

"Yes?" the priestess said.

"My dear and sanctified priestess," Smeme began, "I am a true follower of Athena of the gray eyes, and my friends are true believers also. We are prepared to make good and sincere sacrifices to any God of Olympus. Who do you serve here?"

"That's 'whom,'" the priestess corrected haughtily.

Smeme bowed.

"My apologies, Mistress," Smeme said.

"Very well," the priestess responded, "I serve Hera, the Queen of Olympus, Queen of the Gods, Queen of Heaven, Goddess of Marriage and Childbirth, Patron of Women, Consort of Zeus, the 'coweyed,' if you will. There is no greater Goddess than her!"

"Indeed, that is so," Smeme agreed. "Would it be possible for we, who are faithful also to Hera and her great and noble husband, ruler and King of all the Gods, Zeus, to consult with her today?" He bowed again.

"That's 'us,'" the priestess corrected again. "In any case, what do you want to consult her about… and who is it who wants to consult with the great Queen Hera? You certainly do not look like the appropriate kind of person to consult with her!" she snorted.

"You are right, of course," Smeme allowed. "It is a respectable young woman who would like to consult with Hera. A very appropriate kind of person, I would think! We two mere men will wait humbly outside."

"Hmph," the priestess snorted again. "Who is this 'respectable' young woman?"

"Her name is Elissa, daughter of Yorgos of Oe in Attica," Smeme replied.

Elissa stepped forward confidently. The priestess looked her over with a critical eye.

"I see," the priestess said. "*You* may enter the temple. Come hither and follow me into Hera's noble presence!"

Elissa handed her hunting javelin to Teris and followed the priestess into the temple's main room. The room was opulently decorated, with beautiful wall hangings, elegant gold-covered statues, and ornate jeweled votive offerings. At the end of the room there was a small statue of Hera. The Goddess was seated on a throne and wore a fine peplos. On her head was a gold diadem. In her right hand she held a lotus-tipped scepter, in her left she held a pomegranate. Elissa walked toward the statue.

"That is not the main statue of my Goddess," the priestess declared. "She is in the inner sanctuary. *You* may not enter there. Only the sanctified and purified priestesses may approach her. She is too beautiful for your mere mortal eyes to behold."

Elissa looked disappointed.

"But, you may put an offering in the gold bowl on the tripod here," the priestess said, pointing to a tripod standing in front of the small statue. "I will relay your enquiry to Hera and inform you of her response."

Elissa nodded, searched through her pack and found a remaining piece of jewelry to place in the bowl. The priestess peered at it with a critical eye and was satisfied with the offering.

"What is your question?" the priestess asked.

"I have received a prophecy of Apollo, told to me by Hermes, which says that the beast of the anti-truth will throw an unclimbable object in my path. May I ask if Hera, as the Goddess who supports all women, could guide me in what I must do? Does Apollo's prophecy mean that I should resign from my quest to go to Mount Olympus to consult the Gods directly on their laws and wills? Or does it mean something else? What should I do, oh great and infinitely good Hera?" Elissa said.

The priestess bowed stiffly and exited via a door hidden behind a curtain at the back of the room. Elissa waited nervously for her return.

After some minutes, which felt to Elissa like hours, the priestess returned to the main room and stood in front of the supplicant. She frowned seriously at the expectant young kore.

"This is what my Goddess said: 'I, the Goddess Hera, Consort of Zeus, Queen of Olympus, Queen of the Gods, Goddess of Marriage and Childbirth, and Patron of All Women, say to young Elissa: the divine law has been laid down by Themis, Goddess of Justice, Divine Law, Customs and Assemblies, and Keeper of the Natural Order, and it provides the guide to the best way for mortal men and women to live in a civilized society. Questioning this law is pointless and even foolish, as it has come from the greatest lawmaker who exists among the Gods. By following this perfectly contrived law, the best possible life that can be had by mortals will be created on earth. Understanding this fact is equivalent to attaining the pinnacle of wisdom. Doing otherwise results in you looking like a fool. I send this question to the young, inexperienced Elissa: "Does she want to look foolish?"'" the priestess concluded.

Elissa considered the words of Hera carefully. She certainly did not want to act foolishly. Was Hera saying that her quest was folly? It seemed that way, but maybe she had not understood. She would have to think further on this.

Elissa suddenly felt embarrassed. She hurriedly thanked the priestess and rushed out of the temple, her cheeks burning. The priestess watched her go and then returned to the inner sanctuary.

"Did you receive your answer?" Smeme asked Elissa as she approached.

Elissa nodded. "Yes, I did," she replied.

"Then, what are we going to have to face? What is ahead of us? What are we going to have to do?" Smeme fired off his questions.

"I am not sure," Elissa mumbled. "I will have to think about what I was told. Let's walk, and I will answer you when I have figured it all out."

Smeme looked at Elissa's flushed face.

"Yes, of course," Smeme said tactfully.

Teris silently followed Elissa and Smeme as the pair left the temple clearing and reentered the forested hills.

As the team climbed the hills together, Elissa quietly ruminated on Hera's message, her companions keeping watch for the mysterious danger as they went.

Elissa recollected all that she had heard from Smeme and other people: the stories, the sayings, the way they dealt with issues. She also ran over the things she had seen in her life. Kepheus had died protecting her from the savage boar, but this had been seen as of little importance by her family. If she hadn't disobeyed her father and had stayed away from the farm then would Kepheus still be alive today? Was it her disobedience that had killed him? Was this the Gods taking revenge on her through him… through Kepheus's death? Or were the Gods trying to warn her… or to guide her through this shocking event? How could she know?

Now, Hera's priestess had told her that all the laws come from the heavens and should not be questioned – at least, not by wise people. Did this mean that as a daughter, she should have obeyed her father without question? Since slaves were of lower value in the law, it must follow that Kepheus, as a slave, was really of little value, just as her parents had assumed in the event of his fateful death. Then, if slaves were of lower value, it must follow that women were also of lower value than men. Kepheus must have died to show her this truth, proving that as a woman she should have obeyed her father without question.

This must mean that the world really is a terrible place, and that there can be no solution to its evils and deficiencies. If these things, this state of affairs, is what the Gods themselves think is right, then nothing can be done. Slaves would have to continue to suffer, and women would also have to continue to suffer in quiet obedience to the will of men. Only free men would have the opportunity to achieve and enjoy a good life… if the Gods were with them!

If all this were true then what would be the point of a woman existing at all? She would never be free. She would never have the chance to command and enjoy her life. It looked like it was the Gods themselves who were against all women and slaves. Even Hera herself, who was supposed to be the protector of women, had said as much through her priestess at the temple!

Elissa realized that she did not want to continue to live in such a world. Was a noble suicide the only option left to a woman who wanted to live freely on earth? But, then, what would happen to that woman after her death? In the afterlife, would she be doomed to be tortured in the underworld of Hades for eternity? And what about her body? Who would prepare her corpse for burial? Wouldn't all her family disown her for taking the coward's way out? Would her body be thrown outside the town, to rot and be eaten by crows, a sign to all that here lay a dishonored woman?

Since noble suicide was not a viable option, did that mean that she must return home to be married off to some man and live as a virtual slave in his household? Must her penance be, for continuing to exist, to spend the rest of her years on earth as a breeder of children, a clothmaker, and a household drudge? It was like a long, drawn-out suicide… but at least it would be considered a life of honor!

Elissa stopped walking and stood completely still, as if rooted to the spot. Teris turned and looked at her. She was staring at the ground, immense sadness clouding her face. Teris was concerned, but decided to stand and wait without interfering. Elissa would work out what to do.

Smeme had continued walking ahead and suddenly noticed that he was traveling alone. He turned and went back to join the others. Elissa was still standing, peering at the ground as if it contained hidden depths. Depths that could pull you down, to be lost unseen forever.

"What are you thinking about, Elissa?" Smeme asked.

Elissa roused herself.

"Me? Oh, nothing," Elissa replied. "Sorry about that. We'd better get moving again." She started walking.

Smeme and Teris glanced at each other with raised eyebrows and then followed Elissa without comment.

The three traveled through the hills for a few hours, Elissa staying silent the whole time, and then stopped for lunch.

Over lunch, Smeme decided it was time to quiz Elissa.

"Will you be ready to tell us what the priestess said soon?" Smeme asked. "About the beast of the anti-truth."

Elissa looked up from her meal.

"The beast? Oh, that's not important anymore," Elissa replied.

Smeme's eyebrows shot up.

"No," Elissa continued, "what is important is obeying the will of the Gods."

"Oh yes?" Smeme said. "And how do we do that… according to the priestess?" he asked.

"We follow the laws that Themis, lawmaker to the Gods, has made. Her laws are followed to the letter, even in heaven."

"They are?" Smeme queried.

"Yes. And that means that we women must be like slaves to our allotted husbands and do their will," Elissa said dully.

"It does?" Smeme asked. "But I am wondering if that is what it really means. Is that what the priestess said?"

"Yes, it is," Elissa replied in a monotone. "On behalf of Hera. She spoke on behalf of Hera. She was relaying her reply."

Suddenly Elissa broke down.

"But I cannot face it!" she sobbed. "I cannot face a life like that! I don't want to live in a world like this!" she cried, hiding her face in her hands.

Teris jumped up, throwing his meal aside, and rushed over to Elissa. He knelt before her and took her hands in his.

"Don't leave this world, Elissa! Stay with us, please!" he begged.

Elissa was startled by the passion in Teris's voice. She lifted her head and peered into his dark, pleading eyes. They contained nothing but love and concern for her. The revelation snapped her out of her gloomy mood.

"Okay, I will stay with you," Elissa smiled.

Teris's face showed his relief. He kept holding Elissa's hands for a moment. She did not pull away.

Teris abruptly let go of Elissa's hands and moved back. He blushed and looked at the ground.

"As long as you'll be okay," Teris mumbled.

"I will be okay now, Teris," Elissa replied warmly.

The tone of Elissa's voice made Teris look up and back into her eyes. Elissa smiled pleasantly at him. Teris smiled back.

"Well, you two!" Smeme interjected. "If I may ask something, just quickly?"

Elissa nodded.

"You said that Hera gave you a message. Just how was it conveyed to you?" Smeme inquired.

"The priestess went into the inner sanctuary and consulted Hera there. Then she came out and relayed it to me," Elissa replied.

"I see," Smeme said. "And the message said that you should give up your quest and return home and get married?"

"Not exactly," Elissa replied. "Hera said that we should obey the laws given to us all by Themis and not question them. That would not be wise."

"Yes, hmmm, I'm sure," said Smeme, "but what about the unclimbable object? What did she say about that?"

"She didn't really say anything directly about that, or the beast of the anti-truth," Elissa admitted.

"But are you then going to return home?" Smeme asked. "Is that what you really want to do?"

Elissa considered. "There probably isn't any point in my doing that now," she replied. "I think that, by my foolish actions, I must have brought dishonor on my family. It may be better if I don't inflict myself any further on my family and community. But…"

Elissa paused and looked at Teris, still kneeling in front of her.

"…I should try to find an honorable and proper way to carry on living in this, perhaps, difficult world."

Elissa paused again.

"Though, I have to admit that I am not sure what that is right now," she confessed.

Teris nodded encouragingly.

"I can't go back and I can't give up," Elissa grimaced. "It leaves me with only one option: to go forward and suffer whatever that may bring! It is better to die on the road to wisdom than to give up and try to live comfortably at home," Elissa concluded.

"Well said, Elissa!" Teris applauded.

"Thank you, Teris," Elissa replied, "but I can't ask you, I mean, either of you, to go with me. That anti-truth beast and its unclimbable object are things that I had better face alone. These are not the kind of things that you two should have to face! I brought this trouble on myself through my own stubborn willfulness. You are not responsible for what happens here."

"I will not leave you. I will stay with you until the end!" Teris declared.

"Thank you, Teris. You are very brave," Elissa commended.

Teris stood and solemnly picked up his spear, ready to depart. Smeme looked thoughtful.

"This does not bode well for our quest!" Smeme finally announced, and laughed. "It looks like someone is giving us the bad news – an oracle of doom. We would be fools to go on, but I am feeling a little foolish today! I will come with you. I am curious about what that beast will look like… even if it is the last thing we will ever see!" He laughed loudly and prepared to leave.

Elissa and Teris went ahead together. Smeme followed at a slight distance, cautiously watching the surroundings as he walked.

The hills undulated, the team climbing and descending multiple times, but overall they found themselves getting higher and higher. The air was cooler now. When they stopped and made camp, Teris had to keep a small fire burning all night so they could stay warm.

The next day found the team continuing with their fateful journey toward the foothills of the mountains that they would have to cross to reach Mount Olympus. The three proceeded bravely but carefully, continually scanning their surroundings for the first glimpse of the beast of the anti-truth and its unclimbable object that would surely be their doom. They may never reach their goal, but at least no one could say that they faltered and turned back. That is, if anyone had seen them. The area was wild and remote. No one seemed to live there. The team would meet their doom unseen and alone.

The hills were rocky, with sparse patches of grass and some clumps of black pine and Bosnian pine. The team progressed slowly up the steep slopes. They climbed grimly but relentlessly upward. Doomed but never stopping. They did not speak, as they were too busy trying to catch their breath. In their heads, they silently counted the hours that passed before their inevitable demise.

Teris and Elissa helped each other up the rocky hillsides. Smeme hung back, following the pair and watching for the beast.

The team continued traveling in this manner for several days. Climbing was thirsty work and water was scarce. The three often had to pause their journey to search for the little water that was available, collecting and storing it in their wine-skins. In the afternoons they hunted for food, catching what they could: hares being the most plentiful. At night they could hear wolves howling. They were glad of their campfire to keep them safe.

On the slopes the three spotted various animals, usually maintaining a distance from the strange humans: foxes, deer, jackals. They also saw par-tridges, which were too hard to catch, a black bird with a yellow beak and red legs – the Alpine chough, Smeme said – and the occasional peregrine falcon soaring through the sky in search of prey.

No beast had appeared yet, but the three always watched for it, expecting it to jump out from behind the rocks, or the trees, or even burst forth from the clouds in the sky!

As the team climbed higher and higher, the air became colder and breathing was more difficult. When they were moving they felt warm, but at night they had to wrap themselves in their himations and huddle around the fire. Where there were trees, the black pine had dwindled away and only the Bosnian pine remained. The Bosnian pines were shorter here, often appearing distorted by the wind, with lop-sided branches or the trunk growing at an angle. Some clumps of pines looked like they were crawling along the ground. The mountainside was strewn with rocks, and much of it was also covered in grass. Flowering plants grew in the crevices of the rocks.

In the highest areas the team saw groups of goat-like animals skillfully clambering among the rocks. These brown-furred animals had black, slender horns that curved backward. A long, dark stripe ran along their backs to their short tails. Their heads had a dark line under the eyes, tracing almost to their snout. They kept a safe distance between themselves and the strange travelers.

On one clear day Elissa cried out in fear because she thought that the beast of the anti-truth was flying toward her from above. But when she looked again she saw that it was a huge eagle wheeling high in the sky. Its wings stretched at least six feet across. It was dark brown, but Elissa could make out a patch of gold sheen on the nape of its neck.

"That is a golden eagle," Teris said.

"I thought it was the beast for a moment," Elissa shuddered.

"It certainly is big enough," Teris agreed.

Smeme came up to them. "What a beautiful sight," he said. "It reminds me of the story of the Aetos Dios: the giant golden eagle of Zeus."

"Do tell us, Smeme!" Elissa urged.

"We can take a break and listen to your story," Teris suggested. "We have been climbing enough."

"Yes, let's," Elissa agreed.

"If you insist," Smeme bowed and sat down, making himself comfortable.

Elissa and Teris sat in front of Smeme and waited for his account.

"As you know, the giant golden eagle is Zeus's messenger, and it carries his thunderbolts. It is his companion animal. But where did it come from?" Smeme began. "My favorite story, and the one I most believe, is that the Aetos Dios was created by the primordial Goddess of the Earth, Gaia, in the early times. Later, when Zeus was getting ready to fight the Titans, this giant golden eagle appeared before him, which boded well for Zeus and his compatriot Gods because, as everyone knows, the appearance of an eagle is a good omen. Great Father Zeus adopted the Aetos Dios and from that time on it was his close companion. Not only does the eagle carry Zeus's thunderbolts, it also acts as his observer, flying far and wide and reporting its observations back to him. In fact, sometimes Zeus transforms himself into an eagle and then goes forth to see what is happening around the world."

"Could the eagle we saw be the Aetos Dios?" Elissa wondered.

"No, it was too small," Smeme replied.

"Could it have been Zeus in disguise?" Elissa inquired.

"That I could not say," Smeme said. "Perhaps it is a possibility!"

"How interesting," Elissa marveled.

Teris scanned the sky, but the eagle was no longer in sight.

"What was the other story about the Aetos Dios, Smeme?" Elissa asked.

"I do not like this one, but it is well known," Smeme replied. "In this story, an ancient king of Attica, called Periphas, was loved by his people because he was fair and just. He was also a dedicated priest of Apollo. The people loved Periphas so much that they began to honor and revere him even more than the King of the Gods, Zeus. Zeus was angered by this and decided to destroy Periphas with a thunderbolt. Apollo heard about Zeus's plan and intervened on behalf of his loyal priest. He convinced Zeus to transform Periphas into an eagle instead. Thus Periphas became king of all the birds and the guardian of Zeus's sacred scepter."

"Why don't you like that story, Smeme?" Elissa asked.

"I just don't like the idea of a dedicated priest being disloyal to the Gods in that way," Smeme replied. "Anyway, doesn't it make more sense for such a grand bird to be created by Gaia in the first place and then sent as a sign to the Gods that they had support for their fight against the Titans? That sounds a lot more inspiring and believable to me," he explained.

"Yes, it certainly does," agreed Elissa. "What a noble story and wonderful bird. I would love to see the Aetos Dios!"

"It must be quite a sight," Smeme said, shaking his head in awe.

Teris got up from the ground. The cool wind tugged at his hair.

"Yes, we'd better get going," Elissa said, also standing.

The younger pair helped Smeme to his feet and they all recommenced their journey.

As they climbed, they left the tree level behind them. At this great height there was only rock, gravel, grass, and the flowering plants that grew in the rock crevices. Despite the apparent desolation, numerous colorful butterflies flitted across the fields. The team could not find any more water, so they rationed what remained in their wineskins. They spent another night in the open, burning what they could to keep warm.

After breakfast the team set off again. The wind was cool, but the sun shone brightly in a clear blue sky. Around them were the peaks of rocky mountains. The three continued forward. At midday they crossed over a slight rise and a massive mountain peak came into view. It was difficult to make out in the distance, but Elissa thought that she could see some structures near the top.

"I think that is Mount Olympus," Teris said, pointing at the peak.

Smeme shielded his eyes and gazed up at the mountain.

"Is that really it?" Smeme asked.

"I think there are some buildings near the top," Elissa declared.

"Your eyes are better than mine," Smeme said.

Teris looked carefully.

"I think I can see something glinting up there, too," Teris said. "I can't tell what it is."

Smeme shook Teris's hand enthusiastically.

"My dear boy, you have got us to our destination! Well navigated, sir!" Smeme applauded.

"Thank you, Smeme," Teris replied calmly. "I am not completely sure. We will need to check it."

"Of course we will!" Smeme exclaimed. "And I am certain that we will find that it is the home of the Gods!"

"Let's hope so," Teris replied.

Elissa was frowning.

"Is something wrong, Elissa?" Teris asked.

"I was only thinking that it will all be over for us soon," Elissa answered. "The beast must surely be upon us. We are too close for it to let us past."

"Oh, yes," Smeme said. "I was forgetting about that. I wonder what it is?"

Teris examined the sky and surroundings, unconsciously tightening his grip on his spear.

"Not to worry," Smeme shrugged. "I think that eagle was a good omen. And with this brave warrior here to protect us, not to mention your skill with the javelin, I believe that we have nothing to be afraid of."

"I am sorry to have led you into this trap," Elissa sighed.

Teris put his free arm around Elissa's shoulder. She smiled at him.

"I wouldn't have missed this for the world," Smeme said. "Let's get going and we will see what we will see!"

"Very well, my friend," Elissa said softly.

The three continued toward the huge mountain.

7. PEGASUS

There was still some way to go before the brave travelers would find themselves at the base of Mount Olympus. They continued for the rest of the day and had to camp for the night once more in the cold conditions. There was no escaping the wind up here. The next day they walked and climbed for a few hours before they found themselves looking straight up at Olympus. From below they could see the Acropolis of the Gods. It was surrounded by stone walls and featured multiple grand stone buildings on bronze foundations. The courtyards and streets were paved in pure gold. The grandest of all the buildings stood at the highest point of the complex: the palace of the ruler of heaven, Zeus.

Elissa raised her open hands to the sky and prayed to Athena.

"Almighty and wise Athena, hear my prayer!" Elissa called. "I, your faithful servant, Elissa, daughter of Yorgos of Oe, have traveled here to seek your counsel. But before I ask for that, I desperately need your support, for me and my friends!

"Please, I beg you, please provide us with some power that will help us to overcome the beast of the anti-truth with its unclimbable object. Without your help we feeble mortals are surely doomed." She wrung her hands toward Mount Olympus in supplication.

The golden gates that protect the entrance to the Acropolis of the Gods opened and a figure stepped out. The three sister goddesses of the seasons who guarded the gates, the Horae, stood back to let the figure pass. It nodded to them and flew into the sky and then down toward the three travelers. As it got closer, the three could see that it was Athena, in person. She landed on her feet gently, standing tall above the party.

Athena had not brought her shield or spear, nor had she donned her golden helmet, but she was still wearing armor over her long peplos. Teris and Smeme flung themselves onto the ground before the mighty Goddess. Athena looked down at Elissa with a sympathetic expression.

"What is it that you are asking about, my child?" Athena inquired.

Elissa looked up at the concerned face of the Goddess.

"What is your will, oh wise and wonderful Athena? What would you have befall us? Do you wish for the beast of the anti-truth to have its way with me and my friends? If that is your will then let it be so," Elissa declared.

"How could it overcome you, valiant kore, when you have already overcome it?" Athena asked Elissa.

"I?" Elissa stammered. "I have overcome it?"

Athena's gray eyes looked down calmly.

Elissa thought back. They had never even seen the beast. Its unclimbable object had never appeared before them. What could Athena be talking about?

"The beast has already confronted you and placed its insurmountable object in your path," Athena explained. "Yet you are here!"

Already confronted me? Elissa thought. The last thing that confronted me was… Hera. Or, at least, the priestess of Hera.

"You met the priestess of Hera, I am told," Athena continued. "She was not a priestess. She was not even human. She was the Goddess Eris. You may already know that she loves to cause strife!"

Athena shuddered.

"It is not your place to know the business of your betters, but I can tell you that Eris was not to blame… this time. She was under the instruction of someone whom she had no choice but to obey, whatever her personal feelings might have been. This being did not like your questioning of the divine law, at least not in the way that he had heard about it, and so he sent Eris to do something to stop you.

"I will permit you to know that not all of us in Olympus felt this way, however! Some of us admired your tenacity. We did not think that there was any hubris in your devoted approach. Quite the contrary. We were all pleased when you overcame 'the beast's' insurmountable object and continued on your way to meet us here," Athena revealed.

"Thank you, great Athena, for allowing me this knowledge," Elissa bowed.

Athena inclined her head in recognition.

"May I ask you a question about what noble Eris said?" Elissa requested.

"Proceed," Athena invited.

"Thank you. If Eris was not truthfully representing the divine law of heaven when she spoke to me, what then is the real law regarding slaves and women in society? Do I have the right to ask that or is it impertinent or even sacrilegious for me to do so?" Elissa submitted.

"You are persistent!" Athena admired. "That is a virtue when coupled with intelligent planning."

Elissa waited patiently.

"Very well, persistent Elissa, daughter of Yorgos of Oe!" Athena continued. "You have earned the right to an answer."

Athena considered.

"In Olympus, we know the laws of Themis: they are also the laws of the natural order," Athena said. "The natural relationship of men and women, and of those who are conquered, is clear. Yet, in my great wisdom, I have to admit that not all is known about these things. There are aspects to which even I do not know the answers." Athena paused again. "It may be that in the future the divine laws of Themis will be adjusted to cover these aspects. I do not know. When my half-brother Apollo looks into the future, which, as you know, is his godly gift, he says that much will change. The vision is not clear to him, but it shows that even the Gods' days may be numbered, though what this means he cannot divine."

Athena shrugged.

"As you see, my dear Elissa, there is much that is not known, even in the realm of the Gods," Athena admitted.

"I thank you, great and wise Goddess Athena, for your candor," said Elissa. "Since you have graciously answered my questions, I will not trouble the Gods any longer and will return home. I will not climb any higher and will leave the respected realm of the Gods undisturbed by a mortal woman's presence."

"You are indeed a true child of Athens," Athena declared. "Since you are so wise, I trust that you will take some advice from me? I suggest that you return to Attica and find a good husband who will rule your household righteously and fairly."

Elissa nodded.

"Perhaps the one who is with you would be your choice?" Athena smiled.

Elissa became aware of Teris kneeling humbly beside her. She reached down and grasped his hand. He squeezed her hand back.

"Most satisfactory," Athena said. She turned to Smeme. "As for you, Smeme, it is good to see you again. You have come far!"

"Thanks to this young lady, oh great and wise Goddess," Smeme replied.

"She is an intrepid one!" Athena agreed. "Elissa, please wait here with your party. I may be a while, so make yourselves comfortable."

Athena flew into the air and returned to the sanctuary of the Gods. Elissa, Teris and Smeme set up a small campsite and waited for the Goddess to return.

Athena strode through Olympus, gathering the like-minded Gods together. The group proceeded to Hera's palace and sought an audience with the Queen of Heaven. Hera agreed to see them in her throne room.

Athena and the other Gods and Goddesses bowed to Hera as she sat on her throne.

"Queen of the Gods," Athena began, "you may remember our discussion of the kore from my state of Attica, Elissa."

Hera inclined her head.

"She has come here to our home, Mount Olympus, to seek our guidance in matters of the law," Athena continued.

"Yes, I recall our conversation," Hera said. "It is good that she and her companions have arrived. I see that the never-explained wind, the unrequested and undesired visit of Phobos, and the, what shall we call it?, *imaginative* prediction of the beast of the anti-truth did not deter them. It is most gratifying," she smiled.

"Actually, the beast did visit them, and its name was 'Eris,'" Athena said.

"Eris!" Hera exclaimed. "Poor Elissa. We all know what Eris means."

"Yet Elissa is here, my Queen," Athena said.

"More power to the women!" Hera declared. "Most remarkable. It is good to see our side standing up to the males."

"Which is why we have come to ask for your gracious help," Athena replied. "I have already answered Elissa's query and she has offered to trouble us no longer and return home forthwith. We thought that, since she has been so proper about it, she and her companions should be spared any further difficulties on their return journey. To that end, I would like to suggest that they could be carried home on one of your husband's favorite modes of transport."

Athena smiled.

"That is a good idea!" Hera commended. "I think that my husband should very much help the travelers. It is, in a sense, something that he may feel he owes them, not to give too much away! I would be *delighted* to present your suggestion to him."

Everyone smiled.

The group followed Hera to Zeus's palace. Zeus held audience with them in his throne room.

"Dear Husband," Hera began, "you will no doubt be pleased to hear that a valiant young kore from Attica has arrived at Mount Olympus, in spite of all the strange events which seemed to have arisen simply to block her way."

Zeus stared at Hera from his throne. He grunted in reply.

"Wonderful!" said Hera. "Since you are so clearly thrilled by this turn of events, all of us here would like to ask a favor of you: one that would match the extreme effort that this young mortal has been forced to make."

The King of Olympus examined the group of Gods and Goddesses standing before him.

"What is your wish?" Zeus asked the heavenly petitioners.

"Great Father," Athena replied, "we have a humble request that we are sure would not lead to any *discord*, if you see what I mean?"

Zeus's eyes opened wide for a moment, but he quickly resumed his bored demeanor.

"Nor any other kind of misunderstanding," Hera added.

"Yes, I am sure it wouldn't," Zeus replied. "I am ready to hear it and, if it amuses me, to do what I can. Please proceed, my daughter," he said to Athena.

"Thank you, Wise Father," Athena said. "Our request is simply to return Elissa, daughter of Yorgos of Oe in Attica, and her friends, to her home, without any delay. There she will be able to live the good life that we in heaven believe every mortal should. We think that the best and most appropriate way for this journey to be achieved would be on your speedy steed, Pegasus."

"Pegasus? Yes, I see," Zeus replied. "He would be quicker."

"Then the problem would be out of our hair," Apollo suggested.

"Yes, it would," Zeus agreed.

"Not that there is a problem," Hermes added.

"No, of course not," Zeus waved his hand as if shooing a fly away. He stood and said: "I decree that Elissa and her valiant team be returned to their hometown by Pegasus."

The delegation applauded the wise decision.

Elissa, Teris and Smeme were sitting around a small campfire when they heard a rush of wind. They looked up to see Athena and Artemis flying toward them on the back of Zeus's winged horse, Pegasus. The large stallion was pure white. Its enormous feathered wings flapped loudly through the air, making the rushing sound the three travelers had heard.

The huge horse landed gently, right in front of the team. Athena and Artemis dismounted. Artemis was wearing a knee-length green chiton and had a quiver of arrows on her back. On her head was a small tiara. She smiled at Elissa.

"Great Father Zeus has decided to honor you by allowing you to ride his personal stallion home," Athena declared.

Elissa came forward and looked at the horse. Its dark brown eyes looked back at her.

"I wish I had an apple for you, dear," Elissa said to the horse.

The horse snorted.

Elissa stroked Pegasus's neck.

"I think he likes you," Artemis said.

"He is a fine animal, My Goddess," Elissa replied.

"We wish you all good speed on your journey," Athena said.

Elissa bowed and thanked the goddesses. The pair of immortal beings waved and flew back to Olympus, leaving the team alone with Pegasus.

Teris put out the fire and collected their belongings. He handed Elissa her pack and javelin.

"Thank you, Teris," Elissa said.

Smeme came over to them.

"I will not be coming with you, brave friends," Smeme announced. "Although you have led me to see Mount Olympus, if from a little distance, my thirst to view further wonders has not abated. I am not ready, yet, to return to my birthplace, Athens, but plan to journey onward for as long as my body has the strength to take me.

"I thank you, Teris, for the courageous support that you gave me and Elissa on this quest. I also thank you for your words of wisdom that will keep me good company when I think of them on lonely nights."

Smeme shook Teris's hand and then the two suddenly hugged each other in a manly embrace.

"Good journeying, Smeme," Teris said.

"Take good care of Elissa, young warrior," Smeme instructed gruffly.

"As for you, my youthful-yet-wise leader," Smeme said to Elissa, kneeling before her and kissing her hand, "I am so honored and grateful to have met you and to have been permitted to travel with you on your noble search. I shall never forget you, the shining beacon in my life."

Elissa looked embarrassed and knelt in front of Smeme.

"Nor will I ever forget you, dear Smeme," Elissa said, taking his hands in hers. She leaned forward and pressed her forehead against his. The pair stayed like this for a moment.

"Well!" Smeme said, moving back. "I mustn't delay you any longer." He got to his feet and helped Elissa to stand. "Godspeed to you both!" he cried.

Elissa and Teris mounted the winged horse, Teris taking the reins.

"Thank you! Farewell, Smeme! Come and stay with us anytime you're out our way!" Elissa called and waved.

Teris gave a courteous salute and pulled the reins, directing Pegasus into the sky. Obeying the command, the winged horse flapped its mighty wings and carried the two heroes rapidly upward and away to the south.

That evening, the people of Oe were astonished by the sight of the huge flying horse crossing the sky.

It raced down toward the ground and landed gently in front of Yorgos's house. The villagers ran to see.

Elissa and Teris alighted from the winged horse.

"Father, Mother, I am home!" Elissa called.

Yorgos appeared in the courtyard doorway.

"Is it you, Elissa?" Yorgos cried, and ran over.

"Yes, Father, I am back," Elissa replied.

Yorgos swept her up in his arms.

"It is so good to see you alive and well!" Yorgos said. He set Elissa down and turned to Teris. "Young man, thank you for bringing my daughter home, safe and sound. I am indebted to you."

Teris bowed. The villagers cheered in delight.

The rest of the household emerged from the doorway and hurried over. Agota came up to Elissa.

"My child, you are back. Let me look at you," Agota said. She examined Elissa. "The journey seems to have agreed with you! Give your mother a kiss," she requested.

Elissa kissed her mother's cheek respectfully and Agota hugged her in return.

"My dear girl," Agota said, wiping away a tear.

Timaios was running around Pegasus in amazement. Zotikos, Celandine and the servants crowded around Elissa and Teris.

"You have returned from your long journey, sister," Zotikos said. "Well done!" He turned to Teris and shook his hand. "Thank you, dear sir, for protecting my sister and bringing her home."

"It was my pleasure, Zotikos, and not that difficult, as I had her stalwart help," Teris replied.

"Indeed?" Zotikos said, looking admiringly at Elissa.

"Whose horse is this?" Timaios demanded. "May I pat it?"

"This is the flying horse of Zeus. His name is Pegasus," Elissa answered. "I am sure he won't mind if you pat him and give him an apple."

Timaios ran to fetch an apple for the magical winged steed.

"The horse of Zeus!" Yorgos gasped. "Well, well."

"He will have to return to Mount Olympus tomorrow. He was only lent to us for the journey home," Elissa explained.

The villagers joined the group, crowding around Elissa and Teris.

"Three cheers for Elissa and Teris!" they called. "Alala!"

Elissa and Teris thanked their fellow villagers and shook hands all round.

Later, when the commotion had died down, the family retired to their home for dinner. As it was such a special occasion, they made an exception to the normal practice, everyone eating together in the andron. Teris was hosted as an honored guest.

After the meal was over, Elissa stood to make an announcement.

"Father and Mother, you will be happy to hear that I have decided to marry at last," Elissa said.

Yorgos and Agota gazed expectantly at their daughter.

"I have chosen Teris as my husband to be," Elissa declared.

Teris stood.

"I have accepted this nomination," Teris said. "I promise to keep Elissa happy and in comfort to the best of my abilities for the rest of my life."

"Well said, sir!" Yorgos applauded. "An excellent choice, Elissa. I am very pleased."

Agota went to Elissa.

"I am sure that you have made a wise decision, my daughter," Agota said, grasping Elissa's hands. "I wish you both a happy life together."

Yorgos had gone over to Teris and was shaking his hand enthusiastically.

"This is a great day for me and my household!" Yorgos said to Teris. "I know your father well. I am sure that he will bless this union."

"Thank you, sir," Teris replied.

"Call me Yorgos! We are family now!" Yorgos boomed.

"Thank you, Yorgos," Teris smiled.

Yorgos laughed heartily, clapping Teris on the back.

Elissa and Teris got married the next month. At first, Elissa lived with Teris's family in his father's home. When Teris's new house was ready, the couple moved in and lived happily there, treating each other with love and respect. The Gods favored them and their household prospered, not the least because they were thoughtful and considerate toward their servants and slaves. Already famous for their epic heroic journey and return on Pegasus, they became highly respected in Oe and its surroundings for their honest dealing, fair yet kindly manner, and exemplary way of living.

And from time to time, strange reports came in claiming that Elissa, wife of Teris of Oe in Attica, had been seen laughing while practicing javelin throwing in a clearing in the forest.